Wearing the Rancher's Ring

STELLA BAGWELL

MILLS & BOON

First published in Great Britain 2014
by Mills & Boon, an imprint of Harlequin (UK) Limited,
Large Print edition 2014
Eton House, 18-24 Paradise Road,
Richmond, Surrey, TW9 1SR

© 2014 Stella Bagwell

ISBN: 978-0-263-23939-3

Printed and bound in Great Britain
by CPI Antony Rowe, Chippenham, Wiltshire

STELLA BAGWELL

has written more than seventy novels for Mills & Boon®. She credits her loyal readers and hopes her stories have brightened their lives in some small way. A cowgirl through and through, she loves to watch old Westerns and has recently learned how to rope a steer. Her days begin and end helping her husband care for a beloved herd of horses on their little ranch located on the south Texas coast. When she's not ropin' and ridin', you'll find her at her desk creating her next tale of love. The couple has a son, who is a high school math teacher and athletic coach. Stella loves to hear from readers and invites them to contact her at stellabagwell@gmail.com

To my sister-in-law, Dorothy Sutmiller,
with much love.

Chapter One

Clancy Calhoun paused among the crowded tables of the Grubstake Café and stared at the woman sitting near the back of the crowded room. Could it possibly be *her?* From where he was standing, he could only see a small portion of her face. But the faint tilt of her head, the nearly black hair that glistened with fiery lights, the way her left hand was subtly punctuating each word, seemed all too familiar.

Why would *she* be here in Carson City, Nevada?

"Clancy, there's an empty table at the back."

The female voice had him glancing away from the woman in question and over to Jessi, a young waitress, who was using a paper menu to direct him to follow her through the throng of breakfast eaters.

When they reached the vacated table, Jessi wiped it clean while Clancy tried to snatch a better view of the woman with the dark hair. Her table was now only a few steps away, but with her back still toward Clancy it was impossible for him to get a clear view.

"Are you eating breakfast this morning, Clancy, or just drinking coffee?" Jessi asked. "Huevos rancheros are the special today and Juanita is cooking, so I promise they're delicious."

"That'll be fine, Jessi. And put some green sauce on them, will you? It's only the first of September. We have some whacky weather going on. It's not supposed to be this damned cold outside this morning, so I need something to warm me up."

"I'll have the cook put on an extra helping of chili," the waitress assured him.

Jessi hurried away and Clancy started to take his seat when, from the corner of his eye, he caught sight of the mystery woman turning her head in his direction.

Dear God, it was her!

Olivia Parsons. She'd dwelt in his heart and mind for the past ten years and though he'd tried to drive her out, she'd remained stuck there, like a painful splinter, gouging him each time he tried to take a step away from her memory.

Recognition flashed across her face and she stared for only a moment before turning back to the man who was sharing her table.

Still on his feet, Clancy gripped the back of the chair, while he tried to decide whether to cross the small space to greet her. But he was suddenly relieved of making that decision when she said something to her breakfast partner, then quickly rose to her feet. As she maneuvered herself through the tables to reach him, Clancy felt his heart pumping like a jackhammer.

He'd often wondered how it would feel to see her again and what he might possibly say to her. But now that it was actually happening, he was practically paralyzed, his mind nothing more than a whirl of memories. Even though it had been years since he'd last laid eyes on her, she looked almost the same, except that her features were more mature, her curves more womanly.

"Hello, Clancy. It is you, isn't it?" she asked.

Her voice was still rich and melodic and the sound shimmered through him like a welcome sun ray.

"Yes, it's me." He reached for her hand and she didn't hesitate to curl her fingers firmly around his. "Hello, Olivia. This is quite a surprise to see you here."

Surprise? Hell, he thought, it was more like a violent earthquake.

A faint smile crossed her face and it dawned on Clancy that he couldn't decide what his gaze wanted to concentrate on the most. Her dark hair and tanned skin were a rich, vibrant color, her eyes like a shimmering gray sea. He'd forgotten just how pretty, how downright sexy she'd been, but now that she was standing so close, everything about her was rushing back to him, jolting him with erotic memories.

"I moved here to Carson City a couple of weeks ago," she explained. "A job transfer."

His mind whirling with questions, he forced himself to release his hold on her hand. "Job? Here in Carson City?"

"For the Bureau of Land Management. Rangeland—you might remember. I work the Sierra Front field out of the district office here in Carson City."

She gave him another smile, the polite sort of

expression that was a display of manners rather than genuine pleasure. Clancy could only wonder what she was really feeling about seeing him again.

"Yes. I remember your classes revolved around land management," he said stiffly. They'd met in college while he'd been working to finish his degree in ranch management and she'd been working toward a degree in land management. Apparently, at some point after she'd left him, she'd gone back to college and acquired the degree she'd needed to go to work for the BLM.

"So how have you been?" she asked.

He started to answer but was interrupted as Jessi suddenly showed up with his coffee. As the waitress placed the cup and saucer onto the square wooden table, Clancy gestured to one of the chairs. "I was just about to sit. Would you like to join me?"

She cast a quick glance over her shoulder at the big man she'd been dining with. "Well, for a couple of minutes. Wes is nearly finished with his breakfast."

Clancy quickly helped her into a chair, then settled in the one kitty-corner to her left.

"Would you like more coffee?" the waitress asked her.

Olivia quickly waved off her offer. "No thanks, I'm all done."

Jessi shot a speculative glance at Clancy, then moved away to wait on a table full of hungry construction workers.

Trying not to stare at Olivia, he reached for his coffee cup and took a long swig. His mind must have short-circuited, he thought. He shouldn't have asked her to join him. Anything he could possibly say to her would only rake up things that were best left in the past. Even so, a ton of questions were already forming on his tongue, begging to be released.

"So you don't live in Idaho anymore," he stated the obvious. "What about your mother?"

Dark shadows flickered in her gray eyes before her gaze fell to the tabletop. "She fought a long hard battle, but she passed on about eight years ago."

Arlene Parsons had been the main reason Olivia had left him and her studies at the University of Nevada, Las Vegas. Once she'd learned her mother had been diagnosed with cancer and needed her care, she'd quickly gone back home to Idaho. Clancy had wanted to wait for Olivia until the issue with her mother was resolved. He'd desperately wanted to keep their romance alive, in spite of the distance between them. But she wouldn't listen to any of his suggestions. She'd cut her ties and told him it would be best for him to forget her and get on with his life. Now, ten years later, he was still trying to do just that.

"I'm sorry," he said, "I lost my mother, too, about seven years ago. It's rough."

Her gaze lifted back to his face and Clancy

could see that the news of his mother's demise had taken her aback somewhat.

"Oh. I'm sorry. Did she go through a long illness, too?"

"No. She suffered a fall. An accident at home." He tried to smile, but painful memories kept getting in the way. "So what do you think about Carson City?"

"It's very different from Twin Falls. But I'll get used to it. Anyway, I'm happy to go wherever my job sends me."

So the BLM moved her around from time to time, he thought. The idea sent his gaze on a search of her left hand. No ring. But that hardly meant she was unattached. Could be the big guy she'd been having breakfast with was her husband.

And why would you care one way or the other? The woman turned her back on you. She'd found it easy to move on and forget the precious time the two of you had spent together.

Trying to ignore the bitter voice in his head, he asked, "What does your family think about the move?"

Her pink lips pressed together. "I don't have a family."

Clancy had never expected to hear that from her. All these years he'd imagined her with a husband and children. "Oh. I figured you probably had a husband and kids by now."

Something stark and resentful appeared in the depths of her eyes.

"I've already tried marriage. It didn't work." She suddenly smiled, but the display was just as phony as the one she'd given him moments earlier. "I've not been near your family ranch yet, but I'll be in that area with a field supervisor soon. Do you Calhouns lease any government land? Or do you own it all?"

"We lease a few thousand acres of government land. If you do happen to go over ours,

I think you'll find that we've taken extremely good care of it."

"I'm sure we will."

The man she'd been sitting with earlier suddenly walked up and stood next to Olivia's chair. She immediately rose to her feet to join him.

"Wes, do you know Clancy Calhoun?" she asked him.

The man, who appeared to be around Clancy's age, regarded him closely. "Calhoun? Are you one of the Silver Horn Calhouns?"

Clancy nodded. "Yes. That's my family's ranch. I'm the manager."

"Well, it's nice to finally meet one of you. I hear a lot of good things about your cattle and horses. I'm Wes Wagoner, I work with Olivia for the BLM," he explained with a friendly smile. "Since she's new around town, I'm trying to show her the best places to eat."

Immediately rising to his feet, Clancy reached to shake the man's hand. "Nice to meet you,

Wes. And you didn't steer her wrong by coming here to the Grubstake. The food is always good."

As if on cue, Jessi arrived with a platter filled with enough huevo rancheros and hash browns to feed a crew of men. While the young waitress refilled Clancy's cup, the other man gestured to his food.

"Don't let your breakfast get cold," Wes told him. "We've got to be going anyway."

"Yes. Work is waiting," Olivia chimed in. "It was nice seeing you again, Clancy."

Feeling as if the air had suddenly been knocked out of him, he said, "Yeah. You two take care."

They moved on and Clancy sank into his seat. But instead of picking up his fork and digging into the scrumptious breakfast, he sat there, stupefied and wondering why this morning, of all mornings, he'd had to be here at the Grubstake.

Normally Clancy had breakfast with the rest of his family on the Silver Horn. By now he would've already been snug in his office, drinking a second or third cup of coffee and listening to the morning farm and market report. But this morning, he'd agreed to meet a fence contractor here at the Grubstake to talk over a project to rebuild some of the ranch's cross fences. Never in his wildest imaginings would he have figured on running into Olivia in this busy café. And to learn she was living and working right here in the Carson City area had thrown him for a complete loop.

Did that mean he might see her again? Dear God, he hoped not. He couldn't go through another five minutes like that. His insides were still trembling and his stomach was clenched into a tight fist. And yet the idea of never seeing her again made him just as sick. Either way, he was equally damned, he thought.

"Is something wrong with the food, Clancy? If it doesn't taste good, I'll have Juanita do it over."

He looked up to see that Jessi had returned

to his table and he tried to gather his senses as she tilted a glass coffee carafe over his cup and filled it almost to the brim.

"Nothing is wrong with the food," he assured her. "It'll be fine."

"I've seen the big guy in here before," Jessi commented. "I think his name is Wes. But I don't remember seeing the woman. Mighty pretty. I noticed she came over and said hello."

"And I've noticed you noticing," he told the waitress.

She scowled at him. "Well, what's wrong with that? When I see something out of the ordinary I take a second glance. And it isn't like you to have a lady at your table."

"She's just an old acquaintance, Jessi. Nothing more."

"Oh. Well, I almost made the mistake of thinking you were human," she said with a shake of her head.

He shot her a tired look.

Laughing, she touched his shoulder. "Okay, okay. I'll let up on you. Besides, that darned Ben Harper is motioning for me. Why can't I have just one morning where I don't have to see that silly grin of his?"

"Don't complain, Jessi. He's clearly human."

With a good-natured groan, the waitress left and Clancy tried to concentrate on his meal. But instead of seeing the sauce-covered eggs on his plate, he was seeing Olivia's pretty face.

I've already tried marriage. It didn't work.

Her revelation shouldn't have surprised him. After all, years had passed since she'd left him during his final year of college. A lot could happen to a person in that length of time. But hearing her say that she'd been married had been like an axe to his back. During their time together, he'd asked her to marry him and she'd accepted. He'd put a diamond on her finger and they'd started to make all sorts of plans for their future together. Then she'd learned about her mother's illness and suddenly everything that Clancy had hoped and dreamed for was over and finished. She'd gone back to Idaho and clearly forgotten he'd ever meant anything to her.

And that's what he needed to do now, Clancy thought. Once and for all, he had to forget Olivia Parsons.

Clancy Calhoun. From the moment Olivia had learned she was being transferred to Carson City, the idea of running into him again had hung like an ominous cloud over her head. She'd tried to convince herself that the probability of it happening was slim to none. But deep down she'd known it was inevitable that someday, somewhere, she'd meet up with him.

From the moment she'd stepped foot in this town more than two weeks ago, she'd found herself looking at faces, searching for a tawny head of hair and a pair of long, strong legs. Yet this morning, of all mornings, she'd not searched the

Grubstake Café. Instead, she'd heard a voice be-hind her. A voice so familiar that her heart had practically stopped.

Oh, Lord, just thinking about the way he'd looked was still making her insides shake. Ten long years had honed his lean features and long body into one rough, tough specimen of a man. Thick, tawny hair had curled around the back of his collar, while beneath the brim of his gray cowboy hat his green eyes had traveled over her with a raw sensuality that had practically taken her breath away.

She'd not dared to ask him if he was mar-ried, but a glance at his left hand had shown no evidence of a wedding band. Did that mean he didn't have a wife now? Had he ever had one?

Damn it, that fact was none of her business, Olivia thought crossly. She'd given up her chance to become Clancy's wife long ago. Her time with him had been over and done with for ten long years. There wasn't a glimmer of a chance that a fire could be rekindled from those dead ashes. And she didn't want to try to start one. Her job was enough to keep her happy.

Through the open door of the office she shared with Wes, she could hear her coworker talking in the outer room with Beatrice, the secretary who kept things in order for Olivia and Wes.

"I got to meet ranching royalty this morning, Bea. And it just so happens that Olivia already knew the man."

"Oh. Who was that?" Beatrice asked, her voice clearly indicating that she was preoccupied with something on her desk.

"Clancy Calhoun. You know—the Silver Horn ranch. Seems this guy is the manager."

"A Calhoun! Olivia is acquainted with the Calhoun family? I don't believe it! She's only been in town a couple of weeks."

Olivia cringed as she heard Beatrice's chair

squeak and then the woman's heels tapping across the tile until they reached the open doorway.

"Olivia, is Wes telling me the truth? You actually know the Calhouns?"

Stifling a groan, Olivia swiveled her chair toward the young secretary. Beatrice wasn't exactly a gossiper, but Olivia would rather talk about anything besides Clancy.

"Clancy and I were in a few college classes together down at UNLV. That's all. I hadn't seen him in years." She wasn't about to tell the secretary or Wes that she'd once worn Clancy's engagement ring. The two would never quit hounding her with questions.

Resting her shoulder against the door frame, the perky blonde smiled impishly. "Hmm. I'll bet he thought you looked pretty hot."

"I seriously doubt it." Even though she was trying to sound bored, she could feel a tinge of heat on her cheeks. "The years have changed both of us."

"Well, from what I hear only one of the Calhoun boys is married now. Rafe, the foreman. That means Clancy is still eligible."

Beatrice was only having a bit of fun. The other woman had no idea that Olivia had once loved Clancy very deeply. Leaving him had nearly torn her heart out. And this morning, when she'd spotted him in the busy café, the loss had whammed her so hard she'd hardly been able to think.

"Thanks for the information, Bea. But I'm not interested in finding a husband. I've had one of those before. And I sure as heck don't want another one."

The pretty secretary shook her head in a disapproving way. "You sound like you've been eating green persimmons."

Olivia tried to laugh, but she wasn't quite in the mood to make it sound believable. "Wrong.

I've been eating brain food—you know, like blueberries, salmon and nuts. That's how I know to avoid men."

Beatrice laughed, while Wes suddenly appeared in the doorway behind the secretary's shoulder. "Hey. I don't think I like the sound of working with a man hater. In case you can't tell, I happen to be a man."

Olivia waved a dismissive hand at him. "You're different. You're like a pestering brother." Which was true, she thought. From the moment she'd met her coworker, the two had bonded like brother and sister, which made working together very easy for the both of them.

He said, "Well, little sister, put that paperwork away and grab your backpack. We've got to do some work in the field."

And it couldn't have come at a better time, she thought. She needed something—anything—to get her mind off of the only man she'd ever really loved.

* * *

That same evening at the Silver Horn ranch, Clancy splashed a measurable amount of brandy into his coffee cup, then carried it across the family room. Sinking down on a long couch, he noticed his brother Rafe studying him over the edge of the latest issue of the *Reno Gazette.*

"What's the matter?" Clancy asked him. "You're looking at me like I've got the measles or something."

Rafe inclined his head toward Clancy's coffee cup. "The brandy."

Leaning back against the cushions, he crossed his boots out in front of him. "I'm cold. That's all. I've been cold all day."

His younger brother rolled his eyes. "Hell, the weather today was pleasant. What are you going to do when it really gets cold? Hang around the fire and wait for spring to come?"

Clancy took a long bracing swig of the laced coffee. He'd always envied the fact that Rafe's days were never confined to four walls, a phone or computer. As foreman of the Silver Horn, Rafe spent most of his time in the saddle, roaming the endless ranges of Horn land, tending the thousands of cattle that bore the C/C brand. He truly lived the cowboy life. And now there was even more reason for Clancy to wish his life could be more like his brother's. Rafe had a wife, Lilly, and baby daughter, Colleen, to fill his days with love.

"Spring is months away," Clancy said. "I'll just drag out a heavier coat."

Rafe lay the paper aside and turned his full attention to Clancy. "Did you and the fence contractor come to some sort of deal today?"

"We did. He'll be starting next week. I told him the area down by Antelope Creek needed first attention."

"Good. That stretch of fence is definitely in the worst shape. Are my men supposed to help with the fencing or does he have a big enough crew to handle the job?"

"Leave it up to his crew. We're paying him plenty enough. That will give your men a chance to rebuild some of the corrals down at the ranch yard before you get too busy with the winter feeding."

Rafe smirked. "They're sure as heck not going to like doing carpentry work. But it's got to be done."

"They can't play on horseback every day," Clancy muttered, downing more coffee as he turned his gaze to the wide wall of glass that looked over the backyard of the ranch house. During the daylight hours, the view would stretch for miles beyond the yard to where the distant mountains created a ridge between the ranch and the state of California.

"You have something on your mind, Clancy?"

He glanced at his brother. "Why do you ask that?"

Rafe shrugged. "I'm not sure. You just seem different tonight."

Clancy released a heavy breath. There wasn't any point in keeping it a secret, he thought. Sooner or later his family would hear about Olivia being in Carson City anyway.

"I saw Olivia this morning."

Scooting to the edge of the couch, Rafe stared at him. "You mean *the* Olivia—as in your ex? You saw her in person?"

Grimacing, Clancy nodded. "In the Grubstake. I went there early so I could have breakfast before I met with Reynolds about the fencing."

Rafe let out a low whistle. "Oh, man. Did you talk to her?"

Talk? When she'd walked up to him, so much had been going on inside of Clancy that he could hardly remember talking. He mostly remembered feeling a great sense of loss and humiliation. No man wanted to be dumped. Especially by a woman he'd been deeply in love with.

"Briefly. She was there with a man—a co-worker. She's living here in the Carson City area now. Working for the BLM."

Rafe continued to study him closely as though he feared his big brother was in danger of collapsing or having some sort of mental breakdown. The notion caused Clancy's jaw to tighten. Olivia might have cut him up pretty bad all those years ago, but he'd survived and grown tougher for it. He needed for Rafe and the rest of his family to understand that.

Rafe shook his head with wonder. "Amazing. Of all the places for her to wind up—right here in your backyard. Reckon that happened on purpose?"

Clancy drained the last of his coffee before casting his brother an annoyed glance. "Not hardly. You know how those types of jobs are—you go where they send you."

Rafe made a palms-up gesture. "But she could

have put in a request for this area. Is she married now?"

"No. Divorced. And apparently no children. At least, she didn't mention any." He wasn't sure how he would feel if he discovered she'd borne another man's child. Cheated, he supposed. "Arlene, Olivia's mother, died about a year before Mother passed away."

"How ironic."

His throat thick, he said, "That's putting it mildly."

Rising to his feet, he carried his cup over to a bar that angled across one corner of the spacious room. If there had been anyone else in the room, Clancy would've never brought up his meeting with Olivia. But out of his four brothers, Clancy was closest to Rafe. Though he wasn't sure why. The two men were very different. Where his brother had always been the first to speak up and the first to lose his temper, Clancy mostly preferred to keep his thoughts to himself and his temper in check. But in all truth, Rafe was the man who kept this ranch pulled together and running at a profit and Clancy greatly admired him for his loyalty to the family business.

"So are you going to see her again?"

Glancing over his shoulder, Clancy frowned at him. "I doubt it. Not unless it happened by accident. I wasn't about to suggest we might meet somewhere and talk over old times. When a man has been run over once, he doesn't want to lie down in the middle of the road and beg for it to happen again," he said flatly.

Rafe shot off the couch and crossed the space to where Clancy stood. "You're being a fool! If the woman isn't married, now is your chance."

"For what? To pick up where we left off?" Clancy countered. "Think about it, Rafe. Could you trust a woman who'd dumped you?"

Shrugging, Rafe said, "Well, Lilly tossed me out for about three weeks and I married her anyway."

"Try ten years," he said bitterly, then wiped a hand over his face. "Look, brother, I realize you want me to be happy. But frankly, Olivia doesn't mean anything to me anymore. I'm not interested."

"Really? Then why did you tell me that she's back in town?"

"Like they say, news was light tonight," Clancy said with sarcasm. "I thought we needed something else to talk about."

"Don't try to kid a kidder, brother. You're not fooling me."

Turning his back to Rafe, Clancy poured himself another cup of coffee, but this time avoided the brandy. "Okay. If you want me to fess up, then I'll give it to you. It was jarring as hell to see Olivia again. Especially with her looking so damned pretty. Tell me, Rafe, you're an expert on women. How does one manage to look sexy wearing a pair of jeans and a plaid work shirt?"

"If she has the right kind of curves she'll look sexy in anything. And out of it."

"Yeah. Well, I certainly won't be privy to that last scenario," Clancy muttered, then turned to face his brother. "To tell you the truth, Rafe, when I looked at her face this morning, it was like those ten years had suddenly vanished. I wanted to—"

"Grab her up and never let go?" Rafe finished for him.

Clancy released a heavy sigh. "Something like that. Damned fool, aren't I?"

"No. You're human. You're remembering and wondering. And the way I see it, you don't have a choice. You've got to see Olivia again and decide for yourself whether you really want to grab her up and never let go."

Frowning, Clancy stared down at the brown liquid in his cup. "She might not want to see me again. And she sure as heck might not want to be grabbed up by me."

"Clancy, you're a good-looking guy. Persuade her." With an encouraging grin, he patted Clancy on the shoulder. "It's almost Colleen's bedtime. She'll be expecting me there to tuck her in. I'll see you in the morning. In the meantime, think about what I told you."

His brother strode away, and as Clancy stood there in the empty room, he wasn't sure whether he wanted to curse or laugh. Persuade Olivia? He'd not managed to do that ten years ago. What made him think he could do it now?

He didn't have the answer to that question. But he was certain of one thing. Seeing Olivia again had proved to him that things had never completely ended between them. At least, not for him.

Chapter Two

During the following week, the weather turned colder, but Olivia had always lived in an area where the winters were long and the snowdrifts high. Being outdoors in less than perfect conditions was nothing new to her. Even so, it was a relief when she and Wes finally wrapped up their work in the field and arrived back at the office and out of the cold wind.

She was hanging her coat on a hall tree and dreaming of a hot cup of tea when Beatrice walked up behind her and whispered.

"There's someone waiting to see you. He's back in the break room. I thought having him wait there would be better than in your office."

Perplexed by Beatrice's covert attitude, she asked, "He? Who is it?"

"Clancy Calhoun."

Everything inside Olivia suddenly froze and the numbness she was experiencing had nothing to do with the long hours she'd spent out in the cold today.

"Oh. Well, thank you, Beatrice."

Quickly, she walked out of the room and down a short hallway to the break room that she, Wes and Beatrice shared with the other workers in the building. Since there was no door, she paused at the opening to see Clancy was sitting alone at the end of a long utility table. A brown cowboy hat was resting on his knee and beneath the fluorescent lighting, his hair gleamed with copper lights.

He was facing the opposite end of the room,

but as soon as he heard the sound of her foot-steps, he turned and quickly rose to his feet.

Wiping her palms against the thighs of her jeans, Olivia made herself step into the room.

"Hello, Clancy. Beatrice told me you were here." Her voice sounded ridiculously hoarse, but she resisted the urge to clear it. She didn't want him to guess how her emotions were tumbling around, shaking her to the very core of her being.

With both hands cradling the brim of his hat, he said, "I hope I'm not interrupting your work. She said you'd be returning to the office any minute, so I waited."

She tried her best to smile as though she was really glad to see him. And deep down a part of her was very glad. But the rest of her was afraid to be near him, terrified that the mere sound of his voice would tear away the protective walls she'd built around her emotions.

"That's right. We just got in. I've not even had

time to unthaw yet." She walked away from him and over to a cabinet counter where a brewing machine was located. "Would you like something to drink? This thing will make coffee, tea or hot chocolate. Take your pick."

"No, thank you. I can only stay a minute."

Even though his presence was unsettling, she felt oddly disappointed that his visit was going to be brief.

Dropping a tea bag into a foam cup, she shoved it beneath the brewer. While she watched a stream of steaming water fill the cup, she said, "I'll be honest, Clancy. I'm very surprised to see you here."

"I'll be honest, too. I thought long and hard before I decided to walk into this building," he admitted.

She momentarily closed her eyes and swallowed before she turned to him. "Exactly why are you here, Clancy?"

While she forced her gaze to meet his, she was

shocked to feel her heart contract, then speed into a wild thump. After all this time, she should be able to look at this man and feel no more than she would for any old friend, she thought.

But Clancy wasn't your friend, Olivia. He was your lover, your fiancé. You curled in his arms and dreamed about spending the rest of your life with him.

His green eyes were making a slow survey of her face, gliding over the curves and angles like a fingertip. When they finally settled on her lips, her breath momentarily caught in her throat.

"I wanted to see you again," he said frankly. "Do you think we could have supper one evening? Or if not supper, then meet for drinks?"

Of all the things she'd expected him to say, this was not even on her list. In fact, down through the years, she'd always imagined that if she ever did happen to run into Clancy again, he'd most likely greet her with disdain.

She hesitated, her mind whirling with questions and doubts. "Supper? I—don't know what to say. Why would you want to have supper with me?"

"We were very close once," he said slowly. "I thought it might be nice for us to catch up a bit."

He suddenly smiled, the first one she'd seen since spotting him in the Grubstake and the expression was the ray of warmth that melted the last of her resistance. Why not go out with Clancy? she thought. It would prove to herself and to him that the past was in the past and the two of them could be friends.

She smiled back at him. "I think that would be nice, Clancy. Thank you for asking."

His eyes suddenly sparkled and the sight warmed her. Even in college he'd been a very serious person and she doubted that had changed. But the times he did display a bit of pleasure, it was a moment of pure gold.

"Great," he said. "So when do you think you might be free? Tomorrow night?"

That soon? Could she possibly get herself mentally braced in that length of time? No, she thought. When it came to this man, two, three, five days wouldn't make any difference. Besides, this wasn't a reunion. It was a new beginning as friends. Nothing more, she assured herself.

"That sounds fine."

He levered his hat back onto his head. "I'll pick you up about seven, then. Do you live here in town?"

Olivia shook her head. "No. I live east of town. I'll draw it for you."

Since her small notebook and pen were still in her shirt pocket, she pulled them out and quickly made a crude map of directions to her house. "It's a green stucco with dark brown shutters. A couple of dogs will be hanging around in the yard, but they won't bite."

"I'll be there." He reached for her hand and pressed it tightly between his. "Goodbye, Olivia."

She smiled and nodded, and yet somewhere inside her she felt tears forming. For one split second she felt the reckless urge to fling herself against him, to beg him to forgive her for being such a fool all those years ago. But thankfully she caught herself before that could happen and managed to reply in a normal voice, "Goodbye, Clancy. See you tomorrow night."

Dropping her hand, he quickly left the room, and while she waited for the sound of his boot steps to fade away, she drew in several long breaths.

Had she just stepped into a wildfire or was she finally taking a step toward dousing the torch she'd carried all these years for Clancy? Hopefully after tomorrow night, she'd have her answer.

The next evening Clancy was in his office

wrapping up the last phone call he planned to take for the day, when his father, Orin, walked through the door. The sixty-two-year-old man was tall and brawny with a pair of shoulders like a linebacker and a thick mane of iron-gray hair. For years after Clancy's mother had died, his father had more or less been living in the shadows, choosing to remain in the house, dealing with paperwork and leaving the ranch only when a necessary business trip forced him to. But something about Rafe taking the plunge and marrying Lilly had done something to Orin. Over the past several months he'd steadily returned to the vibrant rancher he used to be. Now he was back to riding his horse and doing hands-on work with the ranch crew. Not only that, he was starting to date a young woman, who just happened to be a deputy district attorney for Carson County.

Returning the phone to its cradle, Clancy

leaned back casually in his chair while Orin rested a hip on the edge of the desk and pushed up his cuff to take note of the time.

"It's about your quitting time, isn't it?" Orin asked.

Clancy nodded. "Sure is. That was my last call. I'm about to head to the house." He didn't add that as soon as he showered and changed he was driving into Carson City to see Olivia. Except for Rafe, the rest of his family was unaware that she was now living in the area. And Clancy was going to leave it that way, at least for now.

"Well, I just stopped by to see if Jett had finished writing up that contract for the bull sales. Kim said he'd already left for the day, but had finalized the contract. So that's good. I want to use that money for more mama cows."

Clancy gestured to the telephone. "According to the guy I was just talking to you could get thousands of dollars by just signing your name."

Orin's frown was skeptical. "Oh. Who was it? Some cattle broker?"

"No. It was that lease hound—the one working for the mining company. This is the second call I've gotten from him in the last month."

Orin's head wagged back and forth in disbelief. "Even when silver prices were up a few months ago, they were still at the bottom. The effort would do nothing more than tear up our land. Didn't you make it clear that we weren't interested?"

"Very clear. But then he started talking gold. I told him there's never been an indication of gold on the ranch. And that we're not interested in looking," Clancy told him.

"Damn right. Here on the Horn our gold is the four-legged sort. That's the only kind I want to deal with." Orin slipped off the edge of the desk. "Okay. I'm off to town. Noreen is giving a dinner party in honor of a coworker that's moving away. For some reason she wanted me to be there."

Clancy gave his father a pointed smile. "The reason might be that she likes you."

Orin grinned sheepishly and Clancy couldn't help but notice that his father looked years younger than this time last year.

"Maybe. A little." His grin suddenly faded to a look of faint uncertainty. "I'm sure most everyone is calling me a fool for being interested in a woman that's so much younger than me."

Noreen was forty-five and looked even younger. Yet Clancy could hardly fault the woman for that. Nor did he want his father to worry over it. "Look, Dad, that's no one else's business but your own. If it doesn't bother you or her, then it's sure okay with me."

Orin shrugged. "You're still young. But a guy like me—I guess I get to wondering what I have to offer her over a man closer to her age. I'll never look like a—what does the younger generation call a stud now?"

"I wouldn't know," Clancy answered drily. "You need to ask Rafe or Finn that question."

Orin chuckled. "Well, whatever it is, I'll never look that way again."

Rising to his feet, Clancy switched off the computer on his desk and picked up a stack of papers. "Don't sell yourself short, Dad."

The two men left the office and Clancy paused long enough to drop the work on his secretary's desk. "I don't need this until tomorrow afternoon," he told the young woman with short, chestnut-colored hair. "Go ahead and close up the office."

The secretary glanced at a big, cedar-framed clock hanging on the wall behind her head. "There's still an hour to go until quitting time, Clancy."

He gave her a wink. "Then you're getting an hour off."

"And don't question your boss," Orin teased her. "Take what you can get out of him."

Expressing her thanks, the secretary began to shut down the workplace and the two men departed the office building. Outside in the chilly twilight, Orin quickly bade his son good-night and climbed into one of the ranch's many work trucks.

Obviously, his father wasn't trying to impress Noreen by showing up in a fancy vehicle, Clancy thought. As for Olivia, he'd learned the hard way that money, or what it could buy, didn't impress her. If she'd married him, he would have gladly given her anything and everything she'd desired. But she hadn't wanted wealth. And clearly, she hadn't needed him. So what did that make him for wanting to take her to dinner tonight? A glutton for punishment? Or a man trying to rid himself of a haunting past?

An hour later, some thirty miles away in Olivia's modest stucco, she was digging through her jewelry for a certain pair of earrings when she came across a little white cardboard box pushed into one corner of the drawer.

Leave it there, Olivia. Looking at the thing only hurts you.

Her hand refused to obey the words of warning racing through her head and before she realized it, she was pulling a royal-blue velvet case from the cardboard box and flipping open the lid.

She didn't know why, tonight of all nights, she felt the urge to look at the ring. Down through the years she'd probably stared a thousand times at the large teardrop diamond. And each time she ended up choking back tears. Tonight was no different and she fiercely blinked her eyes as she slowly traced a finger over the glittering stone.

When she'd ended their engagement, Clancy had insisted that the ring belonged to her and she could do what she wanted with the expensive diamond. She supposed most women would've wasted no time in selling the gem or, at the very least, had it and the white-gold setting fashioned into a different piece of jewelry.

During her short marriage to Mark, he'd accidentally discovered the ring in a dresser drawer and demanded that she get rid of it. But Olivia had stubbornly hung on to the ring anyway. And now, whenever she felt particularly lost or lonely, she'd look at the solitaire diamond and remember and wonder what might have been.

Taking a deep, bracing breath, she closed the lid and stuffed the case back in the box and the box back into the drawer. She didn't have time to dwell on memories or regrets. Clancy would be here soon and she needed to be looking and feeling her best. She wanted him to see that losing him hadn't ruined her.

Clancy arrived five minutes before seven and with her nerves on high alert, Olivia opened the door and invited him inside. As soon as his tall frame stepped into the tiny foyer, he swept off his brown cowboy hat and her gaze was instantly drawn to the thick tawny waves covering his head. His hair was one of the most striking things about him and seemed to match his fierce pride and quiet independence. But it was the gentle smile in his eyes that instantly lifted her spirits and brought a smile to her face.

"Hello, Olivia."

"Good evening, Clancy. Except for fetching my coat and bag, I'm ready. Or would you like to have a drink before we go? I'd be happy to fix you something."

"Thanks, but I can wait until we get to the restaurant," he told her.

When he'd walked in, she'd not noticed the small bouquet he'd been holding close down to the side of his leg. Now as he offered them to her, she hardly knew what to think or say. Ever since she'd agreed to see him tonight, she'd been telling herself that the meeting had nothing to do with romance. The whole thing was only a friendly dinner between old acquaintances. Nothing more. So what did the flowers mean?

"I hope you still like daisies," he said.

"Yes, I do. Thank you." She accepted the bunch of white flowers, then motioned for him to follow her. "Why don't you come on into the living room while I put these in a vase and get my things?"

He followed her out of the foyer and into a cozy living area furnished with a couch and two stuffed armchairs. Pausing near the group of furniture, she turned to face him and it was all she could do not to stare. Dressed in a dark green shirt, dark jeans and a brown leather jacket, he was the epitome of a rugged rancher and far more captivating than the college guy she'd fallen in love with.

"Have a seat if you like," she said in the most

casual voice she could muster. "I'll only be a minute."

"I'm fine standing," he assured her. "Take your time."

Olivia left the room to deal with the flowers and returned moments later wearing a camel-colored coat and clutching a red handbag that matched her high heels. Clancy was still standing where she'd left him, his hat in his hand.

"All set," she said.

He levered the hat down over his forehead. "Do you need to tend to anything before we leave? The dogs?"

"They've already been fed and I let them run loose. I have a cat, too. But she's hiding under the bed. Except for me, Cleo hates people. As soon as she hears another human voice, she's gone."

"Nice cat," he said.

She walked past him on the way to the foyer and he followed in her footsteps.

"At least I don't have to worry about anyone taking her away from me."

"No. That shouldn't be a worry."

After she locked the door behind him, they stepped off the porch and crossed the short distance to his waiting truck. A brisk north wind stung Olivia's cheeks and prompted her to flip up the collar on her coat.

When they reached his vehicle, she noticed the diesel engine was idling and ready to go. He quickly helped her into the warm cab and as soon as he buckled himself beneath the steering wheel, he turned the big, dual-wheeled truck toward town.

As they barreled down the graveled county road, he said, "I think we're in for some nasty weather."

"That's what the long-range forecast is predicting," Olivia replied. "We have a lot of fieldwork to do this month. It would help if the snow held off for a while, but I understand this area is in extreme drought. You definitely need the snow."

"The ranchers around here are praying for a wet winter."

"Then I'll pray for the snow to come, too. Everything suffers during a drought."

"You live farther out of town than I expected," he commented. "Do you like it out here?"

When she'd first met Clancy in college, he'd already grown into a tall young man, but the rest of him had been very lean and wiry. The passing years had filled out his shoulders, arms and legs. Now he looked strong enough to take on a raging bull by the horns, Olivia thought, as she watched him deftly maneuver the truck around a washed-out piece of road.

"I do. I never know when my job might force me to transfer to another place, but I'm hoping I'll get to sink roots here. That's why I took a chance and bought property instead of renting. The house is nothing fancy, but I got forty acres with the place, so that makes up for the price I had to pay. Anyway, I like it out here on the edge of the desert. I can see for miles. I do wish I had more than one shade tree, though. I suppose whoever built the place wasn't into landscaping."

He glanced at her. "What are you going to do with the forty acres? Run a few cattle?"

She shook her head. "It's too barren to sustain more than five head. That wouldn't be worth the effort. But I have thought of getting a couple of horses. I could use them at work. Sometimes we have to ride over a lot of country that can't be traveled by truck or four-wheeler."

He grinned. "Well, I can tell you where some pretty good horses are for sale. You might even get a good deal on a pair of them."

A wan smile touched her lips. "I seriously doubt I could afford anything from the Silver Horn. I don't need high-powered breeding, anyway. Just gentle, sturdy animals that can carry me over the rocks around here."

"I said you'd get a discount," he pointed out.

She sighed. Years ago, Clancy hadn't really understood the differences between them. How could she make him see that he still didn't understand? Even with a discount, a Silver Horn horse would be thousands of dollars she didn't have.

Deciding it was best to ignore that issue, she simply said, "Thanks. I'll keep that in mind." Turning her head toward the passenger window and away from his rugged profile, she stared out at the shadowy landscape and wondered if he was feeling the same tension between them that she was feeling. "When I left Idaho, I was still living in the house my mother left to me. Moving away from it has been—a little traumatic."

"That was near Twin Falls, right?"

She glanced his way. "You remembered."

"I remember most everything about you, Olivia."

His comment was so unsettling that she didn't make any sort of reply. After all, it was the same with her. She remembered everything about him, too. She just wasn't brave enough to admit it to him.

Clancy took her to Bonito's, a rustic Mexican restaurant located on the edge of the city. From their table by the window, the twinkling lights of the city stretched for miles toward the west and the mountains that rimmed Lake Tahoe. Meanwhile, just outside the wall of glass, a Joshua tree and a spiny barrel cactus framed the view.

"Do you eat here often?" Olivia asked as the two of them munched on the chips and salsa the waiter had left behind.

The eating area was rather small and nearly all the tables were occupied. Piped mariachi music was playing quietly in the background, although Clancy had informed her that a live mariachi band played on the weekends. The plastered walls were cracked in some places and the board planked floor had been there for so long that some of the nail heads had been worn away. It was just the type of place that Olivia liked and Clancy knew it.

"No. I don't eat out much," he said. "Greta, our house cook, always has nice meals fixed for the family. And I don't leave the ranch unless I have a reason to."

"Hmm. I guess I must have been one of those reasons tonight."

He cocked a brow at her. "You could put it that way."

Dropping her gaze from his face, she took a sip from her water glass. "You never were much of a social person. That hasn't changed?"

"I'm not a hermit. I get out occasionally. But the ranch takes up most of my time."

While they'd been engaged, Olivia had never carefully measured her words before she'd spoken them to Clancy. She'd felt free to say anything, about any subject. Now their past together was getting in the way, blocking the things that would have otherwise come naturally to her lips.

She said, "I'm sure it does. From what I hear, your family's ranch has grown even bigger than what it was when you and I—when we were in college."

The faint grimace on his face told her that he hadn't missed the abrupt change of her words and suddenly Olivia realized how cowardly she was being. There was no point in trying to evade or dance around the issue of their past. It had happened. It couldn't be changed. So there was no purpose in making herself miserable by trying to pretend otherwise.

He said, "Yes. It's grown. My grandfather is still purchasing land whenever it becomes available. And like I told you the other day, we lease, too. Our lease land has also increased. So that means with more land, Dad wants more cattle. It's a circle that goes around with my grandfather and father. And I have to try to keep up with the business ends of their deals."

She smiled faintly. "That's what you got your degree for. Now you're putting it to use. I'm sure it must feel really nice to be able to put your knowledge and effort into something that actually belongs to you."

Resting his forearms on the edge of the table, he leaned slightly toward her. "So tell me, Olivia, when did you go back to college? After your mother passed?"

Nodding, she said, "She died in the fall, after the semester had started. That was two years after I left UNLV. I waited until winter break to start my studies again. But I didn't go back to Las Vegas. I had all my hours transferred to Boise State."

A small frown furrowed his brow. "Oh. But

you'd worked and saved just so you could go to UNLV," he said. "It was your dream to get your degree there."

When he'd said he'd not forgotten anything, he'd been right. Olivia wasn't sure if that made her feel better or worse. She sighed. "Yes. But— well, some dreams just can't come true. And I'll be honest, Clancy. It wouldn't have been the same without you there. So I—didn't go back."

Even though she wasn't looking at him directly, she could feel his gaze slipping over her, weighing each word and expression. What did he expect to find? she wondered. What did he want to hear from her? That she'd made a horrible mistake by ending their engagement? That she'd been a fool for not trying to hang on to something as precious as what they'd shared?

"Some things just never turn out like we think they will."

His remark shot an arrow directly into the

middle of her chest. "No. Some things never do," she murmured.

A long, awkward silence followed until Clancy finally spoke again. "Is that where you met your ex? At Boise?"

She shook her head. "No. I met Mark shortly after Mom died. I was still living in Twin Falls then and working as a bank teller. He was a carpenter and was a regular customer at that particular branch."

"So what happened? Why did you get *divorced?*"

Because deep down I was still in love with you.

The thought sprang out of nowhere and she frantically shoved it away before she answered, "Because he turned out to be far different than what he first appeared to be. Before we married I made it clear to him that my plans were to go back to college and acquire my degree. He was perfectly agreeable with that until I actually became his wife. Then everything was different. He quickly decided that he didn't want me going to college or having a job with the BLM. He also changed his mind about us having children. He believed our lives would be better without the complications that came with kids. In other words, all the things that were important to me, Mark wanted me to give up. I couldn't do that, Clancy. I'm sure that makes me sound stubborn and selfish to you. But I had already made a huge sacrifice when I left you to take care of Mom. I wasn't willing to make another one."

"Is that what you call it? 'A sacrifice'?"

Her throat was so thick, all she could manage to do was nod.

His gaze locked on hers. "Oh, Olivia," he murmured ruefully. "Why did you marry him when you knew that I was waiting?"

The dark anguish in his eyes was more than she could bear. Jumping to her feet, she blindly hurried through the busy tables until she reached the ladies' room.

Once inside, she dropped her head in her hands and allowed the scalding tears to flow.

Chapter Three

Eventually, a woman with a little girl entered the ladies' room and the distraction forced Olivia to dry her tears and attempt to gather her composure.

Leaving the table that way made her look worse than an emotional teenager, she thought, as she pressed a damp paper towel beneath her eyes. But the only other option she'd had was to sit there and let him see a stream of regretful tears rolling down her face. And she wasn't up to dealing with that sort of humiliation. Going back out there and facing him again was going to be bad enough.

Tossing the paper towel into a trash basket, she smoothed down the skirt of her black dress and with a bracing breath walked out among the diners. As soon as Clancy spotted her approaching the table, he rose to his feet and helped her into her chair.

Once he'd returned to his own seat, she quickly apologized. "I'm sorry, Clancy. I shouldn't—"

"No, Olivia," he interrupted. "I'm the one who should be apologizing. I shouldn't have said that to you. Not here. Not now. Let's forget it, shall we?"

While she'd been in the ladies' room, the waiter had served their meal. One glance at Clancy's plate told her he'd not yet touched his food. Which made her feel even worse. She'd not only embarrassed the man, she'd starved him on top of it.

"You should've started eating without me," she said. "I wouldn't have minded."

"The waiter just brought it. So it's still hot. No harm done."

He looked across the table at her and she could see concern in his eyes. The notion that her feelings were more important to him than the meal surprised her and for the first time this evening, she felt herself start to relax.

"I am hungry," she admitted, then joked, "It takes a lot of energy to have an emotional breakdown."

To her amazement, he reached across the table and wrapped his hand firmly around hers. His touch was rough and warm and incredibly familiar. But how could that be, she wondered, after so much time had passed and so much had happened?

"And I don't want you to have another one," he said gently. "We'll keep our talk in the present. Deal?"

She gave him a grateful smile, but underneath she was actually terrified. Being with Clancy wasn't supposed to be affecting her this way. His touch shouldn't be making her long for more, making her wonder what it would be like to kiss him again, make love to him again.

"It's a deal," she agreed, then carefully pulling her hand from his, she picked up her fork and started to eat.

He followed her example and as the two of them began consuming the spicy food, Clancy purposely steered the conversation to Olivia's job.

"So, are you doing the same type of work here in Carson City that you were doing back in Idaho?"

"Yes. Land management. I worked out of the Shoshone district there. That's where I started about seven years ago and I liked it. But this move to Carson City brought a small promotion with it. One that I'd worked hard to get."

"So, what sort of things do you mainly look for when you're seeing a piece of land for the first time?"

He appeared to be genuinely interested and that was something new for Olivia. The few men she'd dated in the past years never wanted to hear about her work. They mostly thought she just poked around in the dirt and looked at bugs and plants. None of them had understood or cared that nature had a rhyme and reason and her job was to make sure it stayed in balance. But Clancy made a living off the land. He understood.

"The watershed and whether there's too much or not enough. Then we study the grasses, trees and other vegetation to see what sort of wildlife it's capable of sustaining. Of course if it's rangeland for livestock then other things are involved. But you're a rancher, you already know all about that."

He nodded and as her gaze swept over him, she

wondered, as she had so many times, whether he'd ever married or if he had a special woman in his life now.

"Do you ever work with minerals?"

She asked, "You mean land that's being mined?"

He nodded and she shook her head. "A little. Why? Is part of the Silver Horn land being mined?"

"No. But I've been getting calls from a lease hound. It seems odd to me. These days silver isn't worth digging out of the ground."

"Could be his connections are searching for the yellow stuff. Not silver."

"Well, this is Nevada and I suppose there's always someone out there who likes to take a gamble on finding a fortune," he said.

"Yes. Finding it the easy way," she agreed.

For the next few minutes, Clancy continued to focus their conversation on her job and then he changed it completely by suddenly asking,

"What is your brother doing now? Is he still in the military?"

"He's no longer in the army. But I couldn't tell you what he's doing now. The last time I talked with him he was in Oregon, working for a timber company."

Glancing over at her, he picked up a tortilla and folded it in half. "So you two still aren't close."

"No. That will never happen. Todd is like our father. He doesn't need or want to be close to anyone."

"And what about your father? Do you ever see him?"

Her gaze fell to the food that was left on her plate. "A couple of years ago he showed up out of the blue. Said he was in the area and thought he should say hello. He didn't even know that Mom was dead. When she passed, I had tried to locate him, but never had any luck. I honestly think he uses aliases just to keep the bill collectors and bookies off his back."

"Learning that Arlene was gone must have been a shock for him."

Shaking her head, she lifted her gaze back to him. "No. You can't shock a person who doesn't care, Clancy."

"I'm sorry, Olivia."

She gave him a brave smile. "See, I'm pretty much without a family. So I'd rather hear about yours. How are your brothers?"

"They're all doing well. Evan is a detective for the sheriff's department now. Rafe is foreman of the Horn and Finn manages our horse division. Bowie has been in the marines for close to seven years now. We thought he was getting out last year, but he re-upped for another stint. I think he's still trying to decide what he wants to do with himself."

Finished with her food, she laid her fork aside. "Do any of them have families?"

"Rafe. He married a nurse and has a baby

daughter, Colleen. They live in the ranch house, too, so they've livened up the place."

"That's nice. But I'm surprised to hear that only one of your brothers has gotten married." Her gaze wandered across his face until their eyes met. "Especially you."

"Why do you say that?"

"When I thought of you these past years, I always pictured you with a wife and at least two children. What happened?"

He shrugged. "I never found the right person. And you? Do you ever think about trying marriage a second time?"

She hoped her smile didn't reveal any of the sadness she was feeling. "Mark turned out to be the wrong person for me. But I still hope that someday I'll find the right man."

"I have no doubt you'll find him, Olivia."

A half hour later, after they finished dessert and coffee, the two of them left Bonito's and

Clancy headed the truck out of town, toward Olivia's place.

The night had grown colder and bits of icy precipitation dotted the windshield. Throughout the drive, Olivia sat huddled in her coat, staring pensively ahead.

Spending the evening with him had been hard on her, Clancy decided. He'd not wanted or expected it to, but it had and that bothered him greatly. He'd not asked her to dinner in order to put her emotions through a meat grinder. Actually, if anyone had asked him why he'd invited Olivia to join him this evening, he wouldn't have been able to give them a sensible answer. Except that seeing her that morning in the Grubstake hadn't been enough. He'd wanted more time to talk with her, to make certain that the attraction he'd once felt for her was dead and gone.

What a damned fool notion that had been, he thought grimly. All through dinner, he'd hardly been able to keep his eyes off the woman. With a black dress hugging her curves and her dark hair waving upon her shoulders, she'd looked like a sultry vision. Time had matured her face into beautiful curves and angles and shadowed her eyes with smoky sensuality. Now all he could think about was taking her into his arms and making love to her.

When he pulled to a stop in front of her house and shut off the engine, she immediately unsnapped her seat belt and reached for the handbag resting on the floorboard near her feet.

"Thank you for the flowers and the delicious dinner," she said somewhat stiffly. "It was very nice, Clancy."

Her proper and polite response made him want to curse out loud. All during their evening, he'd felt her measuring her words, guarding her every reaction to him. The only time he'd seen a genuine emotion out of her was when she'd tearfully ran from the table. And she'd ended up apologizing for even that reaction.

"You're welcome," he told her.

He unbuckled his seat belt with the intentions of helping her out of the cab, but she quickly reached across the console and placed a deterring hand upon his forearm.

"There's no need for you to walk me to the door. I know the way."

Suddenly it was all too much and before he realized what he was doing, his hands were locked around both her wrists.

"Yes, the trail to your doorstep is easy to find. But do you know your way back into my arms?"

She drew in a sharp breath while her eyes grew wide with disbelief.

"Clancy."

The moment she whispered his name, his gaze focused on the moist curve of her lips and he suddenly decided he couldn't wait on her answer. He drew her forward until her upper body was pressed against his and his lips had covered hers.

He half expected her to draw back or try to resist him in some way. But he was wrong. She leaned into him and opened her mouth willingly beneath his, and as he deepened the kiss, his brain went haywire. The only commands it could follow were the urgings of his body telling him to keep kissing her over and over.

His senses were so lost, he didn't know how much time had passed before one of her hands fluttered against his chest and she eased her lips away from his. The loss of their soft warmth was a shock to his senses and Clancy opened his eyes to see her face was a picture of astonishment.

"Olivia, I—"

Before she could finish, she turned away from him and jerked the door latch. "I'm going in!"

Even though she'd not mentioned him joining her, Clancy practically leaped out of the truck and rounded the cab so that he could help her to the ground.

Once she was standing next to him, he continued to hold on to her elbow. Cold wind whipped across the hood of the truck and spattered them with bits of snow, but Clancy barely felt it. His body still felt like a roaring furnace. "I think we need to talk about this, Olivia."

"What is there to talk about? Nothing. This is it. I'm not going to go out with you again," she said flatly.

With his hand still on her arm, he urged her toward the house. "Let's go inside and get out of this weather."

Thankfully, she didn't protest. Instead she turned and made a dash for the house with Clancy following close on her heels. Once they were inside, she stopped in the middle of the living room and began removing her coat. Clancy quickly stepped forward to help her and for a moment, as he lifted the coat from her shoulders, he wondered how it would feel to always be privy to her closeness, to know that each night of their lives she'd be lying by his side, warming his body. Or would he constantly be wondering how soon it would be before she left him again?

"I can make us more coffee if you'd like a cup," she suggested.

She was still trying to be polite and keep a cool distance between them. The idea was ridiculous and annoyed the heck out of Clancy, especially after she'd kissed him with such feeling.

He handed the coat to her. "Who are you trying to fool, Olivia? Me or yourself?"

She tossed the garment over the arm of the couch, then turned a confused look on him. "What are you talking about?"

He shook his head. "You just kissed me like you wanted to set me on fire. Now you act like we ought to sit down over a cup of coffee and discuss the weather."

She closed the small space between them and he could see hot color staining her cheeks, but whether it was from anger or embarrassment, he had no way of knowing.

"It might as well be the weather, Clancy. Because that kiss—well, that was a onetime thing. Just chalk it up to old memories and leave it at that."

Amazed by her response, he asked, "Leave it? Just like that?"

Her lips pressed to a thin line as she glanced away from him. "Why did you invite me out tonight, anyway, Clancy? To test me? Hurt me? Exactly what are you doing?"

Groaning with frustration, he lifted his hat off his head and wiped a hand through his hair. "The last thing I want to do is hurt you, Olivia. I—" Unsure of how to explain himself, he walked over to the couch and sank onto the edge of the cushion. With his forearms resting across his open knees and his hat dangling from his hands, he looked up at her. "Okay, Olivia, I'm going to be honest. You asked if I was testing you, but it's really the other way around. I wanted to test myself. Ever since you walked out of my life, I've wondered how I would feel if I ever saw you again. Would I hate you or want you, or look at you with total indifference? After seeing you the other morning in the Grubstake, I had to find out."

He could see her mind spinning as she walked over to the couch and sank down beside him. "And how do you feel?"

Her voice had dropped to a husky murmur and just the sound of it tightened his body with desire.

He blew out a heavy breath. "I think that kiss answers your question and mine."

She didn't make any sort of reply. Instead, she closed her eyes and bent her head as though she'd just been handed a prison sentence.

"Oh, Clancy, you can't be serious."

"I was serious ten years ago. Now I'm not sure how I feel. All I know is that when I look at you I still want you. And from the way you kissed me, I think you feel the same way."

Her head jerked up and her gray eyes clashed with his. "And what if I do?" she challenged. "What if there is a flame still between us? That doesn't mean we should try to fan it!"

"You think ignoring it would be better?"

Her hand curled over his forearm and Clancy felt the heat of her fingers all the way up to his shoulder. It wasn't right, he thought, that this woman, of all women, had to be the one who lit a fire in him, who made him want and dream and love.

She said, "Look, Clancy, I've spent all these years trying to forget what happened between us. And I'll admit that I agreed to this date to-night because I believed it would convince me that—well, everything we ever felt for each other was gone. That kiss was nice. Very nice.

But I don't want it to happen again. I don't want to try to stir up old feelings and then—well, have it all end a second time."

"You say that like you're certain a second time around for us wouldn't work," he said.

"I'm not sure of anything," she said flatly. "Except that I've already had one failed marriage. I don't want to make any more mistakes."

"Who said anything about marriage?"

Her spine stiffened and she pulled her hand from his arm.

"No one," she said coldly. "You don't have to marry someone to make a mistake with them."

It was clear to Clancy that he'd said the wrong thing to her, but damn it, she had his head in such a spin he hardly knew what he was doing or saying.

"Olivia, I didn't mean—maybe saying good-bye would be the right thing for us. But what we had all those years ago was special. I don't think you'll deny that. If some of those feelings are still there, we need to see where they might take us. If it turns out that all we have between us is a pile of dead ashes, then we can part knowing that we're not losing anything."

Groaning with anguish, she rose from the couch and walked across the room. Pausing in front of the picture window, she said, "And what if we rekindled our romance, Clancy? Where could that possibly lead us?" Glancing over her shoulder at him, she shook her head. "No. You'll always resent me for leaving you and going to my mother. And—"

Before she could finish, he jumped to his feet and hurried over to her. "Get this straight, Olivia, I never had an issue with you going to help your mother. Dear God, I'm not heartless. She needed you. It's the fact that you used her as an excuse to end our engagement. And then once she was gone, you chose not to contact me. Instead, you married another man. Why?"

Outrage clamped her jaws tight. "I'm not going

to talk with you about that tonight! It's none of your business. When I married Mark, you and I were already finished."

"No! You were already finished, Olivia. Like a damned fool I was still hanging on, hoping that once things were resolved with your mother, you'd come to me. You cut me out of your life then and you obviously want to keep me cut out now. I should be able to get that through my head. But for some reason I can't."

Bending her head, she instantly twisted her back to him. "I don't know, Clancy," she said in a low, hoarse voice. "Maybe someday you'll see that I'm not your kind. I never was and never will be."

"If that's what you think, then I'm wasting my time here. Goodbye, Olivia. I hope you enjoy your new home in Carson City," he said bitterly, then turned and hurried out of the house before he could say something he might regret for the rest of his life.

* * *

Throughout the next week, the weather turned bitterly cold and Olivia had to deal with a pile of work both inside and outside of the office. Which was a good thing, she told herself, as she rubbed her tired eyes and tried to focus on the notes in front of her. Trudging through the snow and dealing with paperwork helped to keep her mind off the disastrous evening she'd had with Clancy.

The night he'd stormed out of her house it was as if he'd taken every light with him. Now each time she walked into the living room, she envisioned him sitting there on the couch, his hat in his hands, his hair waved across his forehead.

Seven days had passed since that night and by now she'd expected to have put the whole incident behind her. Instead, her thoughts were being consumed more and more with the man.

If some of those feelings are still there, we need to see where they might take us.

This past week his words had returned again and again until she wanted to scream with frustration. So what if she still felt something for the man, or he for her? Nothing would ever evolve from them. He'd more or less proclaimed that marriage wasn't on his mind. So what was on his mind? Getting her back in bed?

That question had her mind instantly replaying the kiss they'd shared in his truck and the memory was enough to heat her face. She'd kissed him as though they'd never been apart. She'd kissed him as though she'd never stopped loving him. And then, like an idiot, she'd tried to erect a barrier between them and pretend it had been nothing to her. That he was nothing to her.

Oh, Lord, it was no wonder that he'd left angry. And no wonder that after all these days she was still in a miserable state of mind. If she had any kind of courage at all, she'd drive out to the Silver Horn ranch, face him and try to explain herself. But would that solve anything?

"It's time for me to head home, Liv. Wes has already gone out the door. Are you staying late this evening?"

Beatrice's voice interrupted her dismal thoughts and Olivia turned away from her desk to see the secretary standing in the open doorway. The woman had already donned her coat and shoulder bag and covered her hair with a black beret.

"I want to finish a few more notes before I leave," she told the young woman. "Don't worry. I'll lock things up."

"You've had a long day," Beatrice said. "You ought to finish that tomorrow."

Olivia smiled at her. "I'll be finished in a few minutes and then I'll head on home."

"Well, drive carefully. I glanced outside earlier and it's snowing again."

"I'll be careful and you do the same."

With a backward wave, Beatrice disappeared and Olivia went back to typing up the notes she'd scribbled down earlier this morning when she and Wes had visited a section of state park land that was losing an inordinate amount of pines to a spreading parasite.

She was finishing the last paragraph when a knock suddenly sounded on the doorjamb. Startled, she whirled her chair around and stared with shock at the man standing in the dimly lit opening.

"Clancy!"

He stepped into the room and Olivia could see his sheepskin jacket and brown Stetson were dusted with snowflakes, while his cheeks were ruddy from being beaten by the freezing wind.

"I met your secretary as she was leaving," he explained. "She told me I'd find you here working."

Her mind whirling with questions, she slowly rose to her feet. "What are you doing here?"

His expression suddenly took on a sheepish quality. "I wanted to apologize to you."

"I don't understand," she said, her voice scarcely above a whisper.

He closed the small distance between them and as his hands closed over the top of her shoulders, Olivia's heart leaped into a wild gallop.

"Neither do I, Livvy. All week long I've thought about everything I said to you. And I realized I behaved badly. I asked you out and then started beating you up emotionally. I'm sorry. Very sorry. And I wanted you to know that."

Suddenly her throat was so thick all she could manage was to choke out his name. And then before she could ponder or stop herself, she flung her arms around his waist and buried her face in the middle of his chest.

"Oh, Clancy, I'm sorry, too." Tears flooded her eyes and as they spilled onto her cheeks, she didn't try to stem them. It felt too good to finally quit hiding her feelings, to finally let him see how much the past had hurt her.

His big hand came up to stroke the crown of her hair. "Don't cry," he whispered against her temple. "I never want to see you cry."

Tilting her head back, she looked up at him. "I don't blame you for wanting to punish me."

He groaned. "Oh, Livvy, I don't want to punish you. I want to love you. Like this." Bending his head, he kissed her cheeks, then moved on to her tear-drenched lips. "And this."

By now, Olivia didn't care what he was doing or why. The years of longing she'd felt for this man were rushing through her at such a speed it was impossible to think, much less push it aside. So she did the only thing she could do. She tightened her arms around him and returned his kiss with a hunger that staggered them both.

When their lips finally parted, both of them were breathless and for a split second Olivia forgot where they were or what she'd been doing before he'd started kissing her. But then she felt his forefinger gently rubbing the skin beneath her chin and the tempting contact brought her spinning senses crashing back to earth.

"What are we going to do now, Clancy?"

His green eyes met hers and all at once Olivia was overwhelmed with a mixture of fear and hope.

"We're going to start over, Olivia. And this time we have to do it right."

But could they do it right? she wondered. Could they move beyond their broken past and concentrate on the future? Only time would give her that answer. For now, being in Clancy's arms again had to be enough.

Chapter Four

Three days later the weekend arrived with weather that was almost balmy compared to the highly unusual snow and wind they'd endured the days before. As Olivia sat on her front porch, waiting for Clancy to arrive, she couldn't decide if it was the sunny sky that was lifting her spirits or the idea of spending time with the rugged rancher.

Last night Clancy had called to invite her to join him on a drive to visit a piece of property somewhere north of the city. It was the first time she'd talked to him since that night he'd stopped by her office and just the sound of his voice had filled her with longing to see him again. She'd immediately accepted the invitation, but after hanging up the phone, she'd begun to wonder exactly what she was doing or even hoped to do. Actually, ever since Clancy had talked about them starting over, she'd been asking herself if she was making the biggest mistake in her life by getting involved with him again. Or was she finally on a path to all the things she'd ever wanted in her life?

The idea of Clancy courting her all over again should be filling her with excitement and hope. Yet at the very least, she was guardedly optimistic. The past years stretched between them like a wide river filled with dangerous rapids and whirlpools. How could they ever expect to meet in the middle without drowning in the process?

Five minutes later, she was still pondering the question when the faint sound of a vehicle had her two dogs, a black shepherd mix and a blue tick hound, barking loudly and racing out to meet the black truck easing up the driveway.

Seeing it was Clancy, Olivia gathered up her coat and tote bag, then walked out to meet him. As he climbed down from the truck, she couldn't help but notice his long muscular legs encased in denim and the wide width of his shoulders beneath a gray wool jacket. Years ago, she'd thought of him as a sexy guy. Now he was all man and then some.

"Are you sure your dogs won't bite?" he asked as he warily eyed the barking dogs. "The blue tick sounds serious."

Olivia laughed. "Pepper only gets serious when she's after a jackrabbit. And the only thing Pete will bite is the food in his bowl. Go ahead and pet them. They're not like Cleo. They love people."

Squatting on his boot heels, he greeted the dogs and they immediately paid him back with happy whines and slobbery licks on his hands. For a minute or two he gave them his undivided attention, then rose to his feet. "I hope you don't depend on that pair for watchdogs," he said with a chuckle.

Smiling, she said, "I'm not worried about intruders. A thief could take one look around here and see I don't have much worth stealing."

He didn't appear to find her remark humorous, but then it was probably hard for him to imagine a woman living alone in the country, she thought. From the time he'd been born, he'd been surrounded by family. He wouldn't know what it was like to be totally alone.

"Well, I do hope you're cautious about strangers anyway," he said. "I don't like the idea of you being out here alone at night."

Was he suggesting she'd be safer if he was staying here with her? she wondered. Not hardly. Clancy Calhoun would never leave the Silver

Horn for her or any woman, she was as sure of that as she was of the sun rising in the east.

"I've lived alone for a long time now," she told him. "I've learned to be cautious. And I do have a neighbor. He lives just over the hill to the east."

He glanced in that direction only to see more empty land. "He? Have you met this neighbor?"

She nodded. "I was moving in when he came over and introduced himself."

"Sounds like a fast worker to me."

Chuckling, Olivia said, "Ezra Giddings is a seventy-three-year-old widower. And though he's still quite a looker, I don't think he's hunting another wife."

He frowned. "You already know that much about the man?"

"We've had coffee together a few times. He's easy to talk to. And he'd be glad to help me in any way if I should need it."

"I'm glad you think so."

The skeptical look in his eyes had her stepping closer. "What's the matter? Don't you have neighbors that you like and trust?"

"The Horn is so big that our neighbors aren't really neighbors. Besides, I don't have time to sit around drinking coffee with a widowed woman."

Pressing her lips together, she stared past him. "Then that's your loss."

She stepped around him and headed toward the passenger door of the truck, but before she could pull it open and climb in, he caught her by the arm, prompting her to turn and face him.

His expression rueful, he said, "Olivia, I didn't mean that the way it sounded."

"Then how did you mean it?"

"I just meant— Oh hell, I can't explain. Except that I've never had the chance to be like you— like normal folks, who spend time with their friends and neighbors."

"If you're expecting me to feel sorry for you, I don't."

He blew out an exasperated breath. "I don't want your sympathy. I want you to understand that my life is different from yours."

The Clancy she remembered had always found it hard to reveal his thoughts and emotions to others, even to her. And it was apparent to her now that he'd not changed much in that aspect. Yet the idea that he needed and wanted her to understand him was enough to soften her irritation.

"Your life is very different from mine. I've always known that," she said gently. "Why else do you think I told you to forget me when I left for Idaho?"

He looked at her intently and for a brief moment, Olivia didn't feel the chilly breeze against her face or hear the dogs whining for her attention. The only thing she could focus on was the lost, hungry look in his dark green eyes.

"Can you explain that to me?"

Her head swung back and forth. "No. If you don't understand, then it's something you'll have to figure out on your own." She forced herself to smile at him. "Maybe us spending time together will help you do that."

Questions swirled in his eyes, but he didn't voice them aloud. Instead he reached around her and opened the truck door.

"We'd better be on our way." His gaze rambled over her green down jacket and sturdy brown cowboy boots, then to the tote she was carrying. "Do you have everything with you that you planned to take?"

"I'm ready," she assured him.

His hand curved around her elbow, but before he assisted her into the cab, he paused and looked down at her. "By the way, in case you don't know, I'm glad you're going with me today."

The shadows that had been in his eyes only

moments before were gone and the tenderness taking their place warmed her just as much as the hand he'd wrapped around her elbow. "And I'm glad you invited me," she told him.

He touched his fingertips to her cheek. "I wasn't sure. That night in your office we agreed to start over…but these past few days I was afraid you might have a change of heart. When I called to invite you to go with me today, I half expected you to say no."

She did her best to smile at him. "We couldn't get to know each other again if I started out saying no to you, now could we?"

Bending his head, he pressed a kiss on her cheek and it was all Olivia could do to keep from wrapping her arms around him and turning her lips up to his. His nearness stirred her like nothing ever could and whenever he touched her she forgot about the past and the future.

She was in deep trouble, Olivia thought, as he helped her into the truck, then took his place in the driver's seat. But she'd agreed to spend time with the man. She couldn't back out now. Besides, for better or worse she wanted to see for herself if Clancy Calhoun was capable of loving her again.

A few minutes later, Olivia said, "When you called last night, you didn't exactly explain where we're going. Is this property we're going to look at something your family is interested in purchasing?"

Clancy glanced over at her as he steered the truck onto the main highway. Since the heater had the interior of the cab a pleasant temperature, she'd removed her coat before fastening the seat belt across her shoulder. She looked especially lovely this morning, he decided. Even though her burgundy-colored sweater had a turtleneck, it was still as sexy as heck the way it molded to her full breasts. Her long, dark hair was swept to one side and in a single braid upon her right shoulder.

During their college days, she'd never been a glamour girl like many of the young women on campus. Instead, her earthy, natural beauty had stood out among a sea of painted faces, her faded jeans a contrast to all those miniskirts. Oh, yes, she'd caught his attention right off and she was still monopolizing his thoughts today, he realized. Whether that was good or bad was something he had no way of knowing.

Why else do you think I told you to forget me when I left for Idaho?

For ten years he'd asked himself that question, Clancy thought. And for a brief moment back there at her place, he'd thought he was finally going to get a reasonable answer from her. Instead, she'd told him he'd have to figure it out on his own. Why couldn't she have given him an explanation in simple words? Like she'd fallen out of love with him. Or that she'd decided she wasn't ready to be engaged or married. He could have understood that. He couldn't understand her evasiveness.

"Grandfather purchased a few hundred acres of land recently that connects to the northeast edge of the Horn. He wanted me to take a look at it. See if it's capable of supporting cattle or growing hay."

She cast him a bewildered frown. "You mean he bought it without knowing?"

He chuckled. "Whether it will sustain a herd of cattle wasn't all that important to Grandfather. He likes expanding...staking his claim on more Nevada land. If you know what I mean."

"I remember you saying how possessive your grandfather was. Sounds like he hasn't changed," she said.

"Not in that way. He still wants to own and possess and demand. But these past few years he's mellowed somewhat. We've had some un-expected changes to the family and about a year ago, Grandfather had a serious stroke. It took him months of therapy to get his motor skills back."

"How is his health now?"

"Much better. Rafe's wife is a nurse and she keeps a watchful eye on him."

She cast a concerned glance at him. "What did you mean by unexpected changes? No one else in your family has died recently, have they?"

Shaking his head, he said, "No, thank God. But I do have a half sister now. Her name is Sassy Sundell. She married our family lawyer."

"Oh. A half sister. How did that happen?"

"It's a long, complicated story. I'll tell you about it someday soon. I just don't want to talk about it today. I hope you don't mind."

"Of course I don't mind. I only hope that— well, things have turned out okay for her and your family."

He smiled faintly. "It's turned out very okay. I want you to meet her soon. She's an outdoor girl like you. I think you two will have a lot in common."

"I'll look forward to meeting her."

She didn't say more and after several long moments passed, he glanced over to see she was staring thoughtfully out the window. What was on her mind? he wondered. Their past?

Hell, Clancy, the woman probably isn't as obsessed as you are with memories of your time together. Since then she's moved on. She hasn't spent ten years regretting what she lost with you.

He was giving himself a hard mental shake when the sound of her voice jerked him out of his lost thoughts.

"You've not mentioned your maternal grandparents," she said. "Do they still live around Virginia City?"

"They do. Unfortunately I don't get to see them as much as I'd like. The ranch keeps me tied up and they don't come over this way too often. But I do visit with them fairly often on the phone and they're both doing well."

"Tuck and Alice Reeves are their names, right?"

He'd not expected her to remember where his maternal grandparents lived, much less their names. "That's right. I'm surprised you remember. Especially since you never met them."

"You never met my brother or mother, either. But you remember their names," she pointed out.

"But you only had two family members for me to remember. I have a whole slew of them."

She sighed and Clancy noticed there was a wistful note to the sound.

"Do you realize how lucky you are, Clancy?"

The corners of his mouth turned downward. "Lucky how? Because I was born into wealth?"

From the corner of his eye, he could see her head jerk toward him, then felt her stare boring a hole in the side of his face. Apparently his question struck a nerve in her.

"I'm not talking about money—or things. I'm talking about family. You have brothers, a father and grandparents. All I have is a brother who never considered himself a brother or a son. People like you...sometimes I think you take having family around you for granted. Because you've never known what it's like to be without them."

"Maybe some people. But not me, Olivia. Especially after Mom passed away. Losing her was like having one of my arms hacked off."

He glanced over to see she'd turned her face toward the passenger window as though she needed to hide her feelings from him.

"Yes. I felt the same way when I lost my mother. And crippled or not, we have to move on," she said quietly, and then after a moment, she turned her head back to him. "You say your mother had an accident? A fall?"

"Yes. She lost her footing on the stairs and struck her head during the tumble. At first it didn't seem serious. She had a little bump and a cut on her scalp. Dad insisted on taking her to the hospital and they did a scan on her head. It came back clean, but the doctor kept her in the hospital for a couple of days because she had a slight concussion. She was home for two, maybe three days after that when she suddenly collapsed and died. A blood clot had formed in her brain."

"How tragic," she murmured, then shook her head. "All that time I was home with my mother, watching her die a bit more each day, I never thought that you might be going through something similar. I guess I was too busy thinking I was the only one going through such troubles. I'm sorry, Clancy. Really sorry."

He kept his gaze on the highway and wished there was at least one more vehicle traveling on the two lanes to divert his attention.

"Forget it," he said. "You couldn't have known."

"No. But maybe I should have."

Was she trying to tell him she should've stayed in touch with him? That cutting him completely out of her life was wrong? He wanted to fire the questions at her. Instead, he tucked them away and tried to focus his thoughts on today and tomorrow. Not yesterday.

"Like you said, we have to move on," he said, "and today is too pretty to think about such sad things."

She glanced over at him and smiled. "Today is beautiful," she agreed, "and we need to enjoy it. Together."

Together. That was a word that Clancy hadn't used in years to connect himself to Olivia or any woman. And he wasn't yet ready to use it now. Being in Olivia's company again was good. He couldn't deny that. He wanted to be with her. But he was far from ready or willing to hand his heart over to her again. He'd loved her once.

And in the coming days he might learn that once might be more than enough.

For the next forty minutes they traveled north until the desert floor and the few houses scattered along the way began to disappear completely and the highway carried them upward into steep, pine-covered mountains. After a few more minutes of winding curves that led into a deep canyon, Clancy turned the truck onto a narrow graveled road.

As the bumpy trail climbed higher, Olivia gazed around at the rocky slopes covered with tall green pines and thick underbrush. "Since I've come to work for this district, this is one area I've not seen. It's very pretty and definitely remote. We haven't seen a house or any kind of civilization for several miles now. Do you know how far this road goes?"

"No idea. When we turned off the highway, we entered Calhoun property and Grandfather told me it consists of twelve hundred acres. So this road could go for at least another mile and a half."

"Twelve hundred acres! I thought you said it was a few hundred," she exclaimed.

"For Grandfather that is a few," he said with a chuckle, then added, "We'll go a bit farther, then stop for a break. Greta packed a basket for us. I don't know what we'll find in it, but I'm sure she's put in coffee and something sweet."

"That sounds good. I'll definitely be ready to stretch my legs," she told him.

Eventually the road turned into little more than a dim wagon trail full of boulders and washed out gullies. Clancy pushed the four-wheel drive truck as far and as safely as it could go before he pulled to one side and killed the engine.

"We'd better stop here," he said. "I'll get the snacks and we'll find somewhere to sit. Or would you rather stay in the truck?"

She shot him a disbelieving look. "Me? Stay

in the truck? The outdoors is my passion, Mr. Calhoun. And it looks to me like we're almost to the crest of this mountain. If we hike to the top we might get a better look at the land down below."

She started to open the door, but he quickly reached over and grabbed her hand. Apparently surprised by his move, she stared at him with wide, questioning eyes.

"Before we go, Olivia, I…well, it just occurred to me that you might think I invited you to join me today just to get your take on Grandfather's property." Her hand was warm and soft in his and he couldn't stop his thumb from rubbing gentle circles over the top of it. "I mean from your professional prospective."

Her lashes fluttered. "I'm flattered that you think my opinion of the land has any value."

"I've always valued your opinion, Olivia," he said lowly.

Her gaze dropped to the hand he was holding

captive. "Well, I'll be honest, it never occurred to me that you asked me on this trip today just for my opinion."

"Good. Because I didn't. I only wanted your company, that's all."

She lifted her gaze back to his and suddenly he found himself studying the varying gray flecks in her eyes, the fine pores of her soft skin and the moist sheen on her lower lip. The urge to kiss her was like a strong hand at the back of his neck, trying its best to shove his mouth closer to hers. But he fought against the impulse while telling himself he needed to slow down. He needed to learn the kind of woman Olivia had become in the years they'd been apart before he let himself make love to her. And even then, she might not want to get that close to him again. Not emotionally or physically.

"And that's why I came," she replied.

She was making it damned hard to keep his senses together, but he finally managed to drop her hand, then reach for his coat lying in the backseat. "Well, we—uh, better get started."

Outside the truck, Olivia pulled a black knit cap over her dark hair and a pair of matching gloves onto her hands. By the time she'd wrapped a heavy scarf of black wool more tightly around her neck, Clancy was waiting a few steps away, a pair of leather saddlebags slung over his forearm.

The hike up to the crest of the mountain was steep and rocky in places. Clancy hung a step behind her and several times grabbed her arm to steady her. Olivia could have told him she was well accustomed to climbing over rough terrain and didn't need his help, but for once it was nice to be treated like a woman and even nicer to have Clancy touching her.

It took more than ten minutes before they finally reached a small plateau covered in tall brown grass and a few gnarled juniper trees.

Olivia took one look around, then gasped with delight as she unexpectedly spotted a body of water.

"Oh, my, Clancy! Look down there!" She pointed down the west side of the mountain. "See, between that open space of the pine boughs. The sun is glistening off water. Maybe it's a small lake! Let's go see!"

Before he could answer, she was quickly scrambling down the hillside, sliding most of the way on her rump over the slick beds of pine needles. She was standing on a flat rock, gazing out at the small span of deep blue water when Clancy walked up and stood at her side.

"A pond! This is incredible," he said. "Is it natural, you think?"

Funny, but exploring land and studying its surface was her job and she was accustomed to seeing everything from ugly to heavenly. But standing here with Clancy, seeing this place through his eyes made it all seem special, as though they were looking down on the most beautiful place on earth.

Watch it, Olivia. Just because Clancy looks like a prince in a cowboy hat, doesn't mean he can make all your fairy tales come true.

Careful to keep her eyes on the view in front of them, she answered, "I don't think so. I'll bet if we walk around to the other side, we'll see where a stream has been dammed."

"Hmm. By nature or humans?" He glanced back up the mountainside. "And where is the water coming from? I don't see a creek or stream feeding it."

"Let's go see if we can figure it out," she suggested.

He left the saddlebags on the rock and they descended the steep terrain until they could skirt the water's edge. Halfway around the elongated pool, they found a dam spanning a ten- or twelve-foot distance. The enormous moss-covered logs were jammed between two large boulders and had apparently been there far more years than she or Clancy had been alive.

"Wow, this looks really old," she exclaimed. "How in the world did they build it? With machinery, you think?"

"My guess would be with men and mules."

"It does look that old," Olivia agreed, then gazed across the span of water. "And I'm guessing this pool is probably fed by a spring in the side of the mountain. Otherwise it wouldn't be this full."

"You're probably right. Water is leaking from beneath the bottom of the dam and we've just gone through an extremely dry summer. Something is keeping this pool filled to the brim."

"Someone went to a lot of work to have water up here," Clancy stated, clearly intrigued by their find. "Maybe there's an old house below."

She cast him an eager look. "Let's walk down

the mountain and explore a bit. If there is an old homestead around, I'd like to see it."

"Me, too," he said.

The two of them started down the hillside when they suddenly came up on pieces of bleached lumber strewn in the grass. Some of the pieces were still held together by rusty nails, while others had rotted away to little more than shards of wood.

"Something was here at one time," Olivia said, "but this isn't enough lumber to have ever been a house."

"Doesn't appear to be." He reached down and picked up two wide boards that made a V shape. "This looks like an old flume to me, Olivia."

She considered his suggestion as she looked thoughtfully up the hillside toward the pool of water. "That's it, Clancy. That's what the water was for. To wash ore. But where was the ore coming from? I don't see—" She broke off as he pointed to a spot behind her right shoulder.

"Look behind you."

Olivia turned and after a careful scan of the scrubby hillside, she spotted a small opening partially hidden behind the limbs of a spruce tree.

"A mine!" she cried excitedly.

"Olivia, wait!"

Ignoring his command, she raced around the edge of the pond and quickly picked her way down the embankment, through rock and brush, until she reached a ledge below. Clancy hurried to keep up with her and just as she was about to reach the entrance to the dark cavern in the side of the mountain, he managed to snag ahold of her shoulder.

His action caused her to lose her balance and teeter backward. Her upper body landed against him and as he was doing his best to steady her, she twisted around and planted her hands in the middle of his chest.

"What are you doing?" she asked with breath-less dismay.

"I couldn't let you run into that thing! It might cave in on you!"

There was real concern on his face and it shook her almost as much as having the front of her body pressed close to his. "Clancy, I'm sorry if I scared you. I wasn't going to run in-side the cavern."

"You could have fooled me," he said brusquely. "You were flying over here like a bee to honey."

By now heat from his body was oozing into hers, setting her senses on a slow simmer. Desire was swirling through her, shortening her breaths and fogging her senses. If she didn't step away from him soon, she was going to do something reckless.

"I was only going to peep through the door," she assured him. "I've seen plenty of these old mines during my work with the BLM. They're treacherous. I know better than to go inside one."

He sighed with relief, but his hands remained clamped upon her shoulders and Olivia wondered if the same desire that was stirring in her was working its way through him.

Frowning, he said, "I should've realized you weren't going to do something dumb. But I… don't want anything to happen to you, Olivia."

Sunlight was flickering through the pines over their heads, dappling his features with lights and shadows. The angles and curves of his face hadn't changed much since they'd been apart, she decided. Except that time had hardened his jaw and the line of his mouth. The lure of the latter had her heart hammering, her breath catching painfully in her throat.

"What are we doing, Clancy?"

His hands eased their grip to slide slowly, seductively against her back.

"What do you mean?"

Her throat thickened and made her voice

hoarse when she spoke. "Why are we here to-gether? Pretending that we can start over?"

His hands urged her even closer and Olivia suddenly hated the thickness of her coat. She wanted to shove away the puffy fabric separating their bodies and crush herself against him.

"Pretending?" he countered. "What makes you think we can't start over?"

A tiny groan sounded in her throat before she glanced away. "Because I don't think we ever really ended."

Long, silent moments ticked by before he brought a finger beneath her chin and tugged her face back around to his.

"What did you say?" he asked.

"You heard me."

"Yes. But I want to hear it again."

She drew in a deep breath and repeated her words. "I don't think we ever really ended."

His head moved from one side to the other in disbelief. "Livvy. Livvy."

The shortened name was whispered with a longing that tore right through her heart and before she could ponder or wonder about being safe or sorry, she rose up on her toes and pressed her lips to his.

Chapter Five

The taste of her instantly set a fire in Clancy and as he wrapped her closer against him and deepened the kiss, he forgot all those earlier warnings he'd given himself concerning Olivia. Caution might be the safe route to take with this woman, but not when desire was rolling through him, dragging him along at a speed too fast to brake.

Somewhere in the back of his mind, he heard the wind whistling through the pine boughs above their heads and farther up the mountain, the faint, piercing cry of a hawk. But even those sounds began to dim as hot blood rushed to his head and pounded loudly in his ears.

Kissing Olivia was like unwrapping a gift and each layer of paper he peeled away intensified the pleasure of what he might find inside. And he desperately needed to get to the inside, to fill himself with her hot sweetness.

But just as he started to push his hands beneath her clothing and seek the soft flesh above the waistband of her jeans, he could feel her drawing back until cold air slipped between their lips and her hands dropped away from the middle of his chest.

"Why did you do that?" he murmured hoarsely.

Her gray eyes were smoky as they scanned his face. "Why did I kiss you?"

"No. Why did you stop?"

Bowing her head, she turned away from him and in that moment Clancy realized that what she'd said was completely right. Even though they'd not seen each other in years, the feelings between them had never ended. But what were those feelings? Surely not love. Love would have kept them together. Not torn them apart.

She muttered, "I'm not sure we should be doing this."

His hands rested on her shoulders. "What should we be doing? Hashing and rehashing the past? That's not going to get us anywhere."

She looked up at him and the troubled shadows in her eyes told him she was feeling just as torn and confused as he was.

"And where do you want us to go, Clancy? To bed?"

For the first time in ages, he felt hot color swarming up his throat and over his face. "I'm a man. I'd be lying if I said the idea hasn't gone through my mind. But right now we're talking about a kiss…not going to bed together!"

Sucking in a deep breath, she turned away from him and stared off into the wooded mountainside. "A kiss can lead to a lot of things," she said softly.

He walked up behind her and rested his hands on her shoulders. "Livvy, I'm just as confused about all of this as you are. And I'll be honest—when I kiss you it scares the hell out of me. Because I don't know what's going to happen. I don't know if I'm going to wake up tomorrow and have you tell me you're leaving. Again."

She twisted around to him, her mouth gaped with disbelief. "If that's the way you think, then why are you even bothering with me?"

Shaking his head, he gently cradled her face with his hands. "Because I can't stay away from you. When I kiss you I feel something else along with all that fear, Livvy. It's that same something I felt all those years ago when we were together."

Her lashes fluttered before her eyelids finally fell shut and he wondered what sort of thoughts were rolling behind them. Had he already ruined the tenuous bond between them?

"I guess all of this scares me a bit, too," she finally admitted. "Maybe because I never expected to—want you like this. Again."

She opened her eyes to look at him and he could see confusion flickering in the gray depths, but he also saw longing and that was enough to keep his hands on her face, his heart hoping.

"We need time, Olivia. Eventually we'll know exactly how we feel and where this is supposed to take us. But for right now, let's just enjoy the rest of the day. What do you say?"

Nodding, she gave him a broad smile and he was happy to see a twinkle return to her eyes.

"You're right. We can't figure things out in a day. And I still want to peep into that mine."

Deciding it was past time to lighten the moment, Clancy chuckled and turned her in the direction of the open mine shaft. "Go peep all you want. I'll stand behind you, and keep a hold on your hand just to make sure you don't take a step or two inside."

"You're a real trusting guy," she said drolly.

The two of them stepped over to the crude opening and as they explored around the entrance to the deserted mine, Clancy did his best to put their heated kiss out of his mind.

"I'm curious about when this mine was first started and whether it produced anything," Olivia said as she squatted on her boot heels to examine the rocks and dirt spilling out from the opening. "I don't see any trace of minerals in these rocks, but who knows what might be inside."

While she pilfered in the gravel, Clancy spotted a pair of boards lying a few feet away beneath a thick stand of sagebrush. Figuring they must have completed the wooden frame around the entrance, he pulled them to where a spot of sunlight illuminated the ground.

"Look at this, Livvy."

Stepping over to his side, she read out loud the words carved on a piece of weathered board, "Saddle Springs Mine. Established 1904. Wow, this claim has been here for a long time."

"More than a century ago. Makes you wonder what brought someone to this spot."

"Yes, and if they discovered any gold or silver here," she added. "You could probably search the old archives of claims and trace who owned it."

Clancy shrugged with indifference. "None of that matters. Like Dad said the other day, our gold on the Horn is the four-legged kind. Although, Grandfather has different opinions on investments. He owns some mining stock and it's very lucrative."

She inclined her head toward the entrance to the mine. "Are you going to tell him about what we found today?"

"I'd never keep anything from Grandfather.

Even though he's not always been transparent with the rest of us," he added dourly.

Frowning with curiosity, she asked, "What does that mean?"

He shook his head. "For years Grandfather carried family secrets that none of us knew about. Not until our half sister showed up. But like I said earlier, I'll tell you all about it some other time. Right now, let's hike back up the hill and get our snacks."

A few minutes later they were back on the plateau of the mountain at the edge of the meadow, sitting together on a fallen log and sipping coffee from foam cups.

The bright sunlight bathed the dried brown grass stretching in front of them, turning the small meadow into a golden sea, dipping and waving in the breeze. Beyond the grass, tall Ponderosa pines towered toward the azure sky and shaded the underbrush below.

Sighing with pleasure, Olivia gazed around them. "This would make a lovely homestead, even though it would cost a fortune to get electricity up here. But the person who worked that mine couldn't have been concerned about electricity. That was long before rural power ever came into existence."

"Yeah," Clancy agreed. "Makes you wonder if the miner lived here on the mountain. If so, it would've been a rough life."

Olivia bit off a piece of granola bar and chewed it thoughtfully before she replied, "It was probably rough living, but it would've been exciting. If I'd lived back during the rush I would've been a prospector, that's for sure."

Surprised, he looked at her. "Women didn't do that," he said, then seeing she was about to protest, he quickly consented, "Okay, there were probably a few. But the work was very physical and they were exposed to the harsh elements. Not to mention an ever-present danger of thieves and renegades. A woman like you—I can't see you living like that."

She simply smiled at him. "Maybe you can't, but I can. Life is full of dangers, whether you lived it a century ago or now. A person has to take risks at times. Otherwise, you wouldn't really be living."

He frowned. "I didn't realize finding gold interested you."

She let out a low laugh and the sound caused something to tumble over in his stomach. Seeing her happy and smiling filled him with ridiculous pleasure.

"Finding gold has nothing to do with it. I'm just an earthy woman. The idea of living close to the land has always appealed to me."

He placed his empty cup into a pouch in the saddlebag. "I remember that it was your mother who inspired you to study land management, but where did she get her love of the outdoors?

From what I recall, you said you and your family had always lived in town."

"That's right. But my grandparents owned a farm in southern Idaho where they grew potatoes and alfalfa. So my mother grew up helping them work the land. Some of my earliest memories are going there to visit. The smell of the turned earth and fresh cut alfalfa fascinated me and then there were so many places to explore—the fields and creeks and hills. I would always cry whenever we had to leave and go back to town. That's how it all started for me."

"I take it your grandparents are no longer farming."

With a smile of fond remembrance, she shook her head. "No. Age finally caught up to them and their health began to fail. The farm got to be too much for them so they sold it and moved to a tiny house in town. About a year after that they passed away within a month of each other.

Other than my mom, they were the last of my close relatives."

"What about your dad's parents? Were they ever around?"

She shook her head. "From what Mother told me, his parents were never married and they went their separate ways when Dad was only a young boy. His mom mostly raised him, but he left home when he was sixteen and never went back. I guess even as a child, Chuck Parsons was a rolling stone."

He gave her a rueful smile. "I wonder why I didn't already know this about your family?"

The look she settled on him was meaningful. "Because back in our college days we didn't talk a lot about our families. We were busy with studies and…other things."

Yeah, he thought. It was those other things that had monopolized their relationship, but now he needed to see beyond the physical bliss they'd once had together. He needed to learn about the hopes and dreams that were living inside her now and then try to figure out if he could ever fit in them. Or if he even wanted to fit into them.

Rising to his feet, he gazed out at the picturesque meadow guarded by stately pines and the tall mountains rising high on the western horizon. Olivia had said it would make a lovely spot for a home and she was right. He had plenty of money to build a house on this mountaintop, but he had no wife or children, and living up here alone held little appeal to him. At one time he would have climbed to the highest mountain and built her a castle if it would've persuaded her to marry him. But now the image of her saying goodbye and walking away had left him cautious and wounded. The idea of investing a pot of money in Olivia didn't daunt him, but he was far from ready to invest his heart.

The touch of Olivia's hand on the back of his arm pulled him out of his thoughts and he glanced around to see she'd left the log to stand beside him.

"Clancy, what I just said—I didn't mean it in a tawdry way," she said gently. "We were young and—"

"In love?"

She nodded and Clancy didn't miss the watery glaze in her gray eyes.

"I wish I could believe that, Livvy."

She drew in a deep breath, then let it out. "One day I hope you understand how much I cared about you."

Bothered by her quiet resolve, he turned and plucked up the saddlebags from the log where they'd been sitting.

"Come on," he said. "I see clouds rolling in from the north. By the time we get home it will probably be blowing cold again."

"Oh, those clouds are still miles away," she protested. "Let's walk a bit farther west. We might find something else interesting to tell your grandfather."

How could he deny her when each moment he spent with the woman was like a kid reaching for a piece of candy? It might not be good for him, but he couldn't resist.

"All right," he agreed. "But don't complain if you start shivering."

She chuckled. "You won't hear me complaining. I'm much tougher than you think, Mr. Calhoun."

Did she mean physically or emotionally or both? he wondered.

Clancy hardly needed to ask himself that question. Compared to him, Olivia was iron solid. She'd had the courage and the strength to move on, to try marriage, reach for the job she wanted and ultimately support herself. That's more than the life he'd lived safely cocooned on the Silver Horn.

Annoyed by the mocking thoughts going around in his head, he reached for her elbow.

"Let's go," he said gruffly. "We'll hike as far as you like."

She smiled and the thrill that shot through him was akin to a warning bell clanging in his head. Much more of this and he was going to be promising her anything, he thought. And he couldn't do that this time. He couldn't dive in headfirst, then worry about drowning as the waters closed over his head.

But as they walked side by side through the brown, knee-deep grass, he wanted to pull her into his arms and forget all the cautions and warnings going off in his head. He wanted to make love to her again. And then maybe he'd see that she wasn't the goddess that he remembered, but just another woman. Maybe then he'd finally be able to put her behind him and get on with his future.

By the time Clancy returned home to the Silver Horn, darkness had spread over the massive ranch yard. When he entered the house through the kitchen, Greta was putting away the leftovers of supper and Tessa, the maid, was loading the dishwasher.

As he removed his heavy coat, the longtime family cook glanced over her shoulder at him. "There you are! Just as I'm putting everything away!" she scolded.

"Don't worry about it, Greta. I'll grab a sandwich or something later."

The pudgy shaped woman with short graying hair, waved away his words. "Not as long as there's breath in my body. I'll heat you a plate."

"Later," he told her. "I need to talk to Grandfather before he retires for the night."

"No danger of that happening anytime soon. He's with your father in the family room. Tessa just took them coffee."

Clancy glanced over at the slim maid, who was busy scraping leftover food from a stack of plates. "What sort of mood was Grandfather in, Tessa?"

Glancing around at him, the young woman, with her brown hair pulled into a ballerina knot, wrinkled her nose. "He wasn't in one of his rants, if that's what you're wondering. But I did overhear him saying that you should've been home hours ago."

Clancy inwardly groaned as he started out of the kitchen. He was over thirty, but Bart still wanted to set the rules for him and the rest of the family.

Staying on the ground floor of the huge three-story house, Clancy walked down a long hall-way, then entered a large room furnished with comfortable furniture and warmed by an enormous fireplace. A few feet away from the hearth, his grandfather, Bart, was seated in an armchair while Orin was over at the bar, pouring coffee from an insulated pot.

"Is there enough of that coffee for me,

too?" Clancy asked his father as he strode into the room.

Orin looked up from his task. "Plenty. Go sit by your grandfather and I'll bring you a cup."

Hearing Clancy's voice, Bart looked around with relief. "It's about time you showed up! I was getting damned worried about you! I've been ringing that phone of yours for the past two hours."

Clancy eased down into an armchair that was angled to his grandfather's left. "Sorry, Grandfather. I turned it off. Besides, where I've been it probably didn't have a signal anyway."

Bart looked annoyed, but said nothing as Orin arrived with a red mug of coffee and a plate of brownies. Clancy took the mug but declined the chocolate treat.

"Thanks, but I've not eaten supper yet. I'll have one later," he told his father.

A few feet away, Bart leaned forward in his chair. "It shouldn't have taken you all day to look over twelve hundred acres. Did you have trouble or something?"

Clancy exchanged a subtle look with his father before turning his attention back to Bart. "No trouble. I took my time. Or I should say, we took our time."

"'We'? You took someone with you?" Orin asked with surprise.

"Clancy, that land is Calhoun business," Bart spoke up. "I don't appreciate you letting someone else look it over—especially before I do."

Clancy looked at both men and decided there was no point in keeping Olivia a secret. Especially since he'd made the decision to keep seeing her. At least for the time being.

"Don't get all worked up, Grandfather. It was a woman—a date of sorts."

This news brought Bart to the edge of his chair while Orin stared in surprise.

"A woman?" The older man grunted with

disbelief. "You haven't been out with a woman in years!"

The idea that an eighty-four-year-old man could sum up Clancy's love life in one sentence annoyed the hell out of him.

"Well, I was today," he said curtly, then carefully sipped his coffee. "Olivia Parsons was with me."

From the corner of his eye, he could see a stunned look come over his father.

"Olivia?" he asked.

Not one to hide his feelings or opinions, Bart quickly pushed himself out of the chair. "You mean that woman that broke your engagement all those years ago?"

Bart's demanding tone had Clancy passing a weary hand over his face. "That's the one."

The older man stalked over to Clancy's chair and glared down at him. "What the hell were you doing with her? She's no good!"

Clancy grimaced. "No good? The one time

she was here on the ranch, I doubt you said more than three words to her. You couldn't possibly know whether she's good or not."

"I remember that she whacked your boots out from under you! What are you wanting with her now? For her to knock you down again?"

Walking over to the rock hearth, Orin turned his back to the fire. "Dad, is all of this necessary? Leave Clancy alone. He's not a kid anymore."

"I'm glad one of you remembers that," Clancy muttered.

Bart cursed and Clancy watched the older man rake a hand through his thick gray hair. Even when he was annoyed with his grandfather, he admired the man. His physical and mental strength were still stronger than most men in their fifties. Throughout the years, he'd kept the Horn thriving and prosperous, even when surrounding ranches were struggling to keep up with the harsh weather and an unpredictable cattle market.

"Hell, son, I'm only saying this out of concern," Bart said in a gentler tone. "I don't want any woman to ever hurt you again. Not like she did."

Even though his broken engagement with Olivia happened years ago, hearing Bart discuss it now was very humiliating for Clancy. Had he really been that lost and transparent back then? Like a weak, immature teenager mooning over the fact that he couldn't hang on to the prom queen? He didn't like to think so. But one thing he was certain about now, he'd never let himself reach that low a place again.

"I'm not planning on letting that happen again," he said gruffly.

Bart walked over to the bar, and for a second Clancy feared his grandfather was going to reach for the Scotch he used to sip from sundown to bedtime. But thankfully the older man reached for the coffeepot instead.

"What is she doing around here, anyway? I thought you told us she went back to Idaho," Bart said as he carried the mug back over to the group of chairs.

"She's working for the BLM now. Land management."

"Is she married?" Orin asked.

Clancy glanced over at his father. "She's divorced. No children. Her mother died about the same time Mom died."

With a rueful shake of his head, he said, "I'm sorry to hear that. So is she living around here now?"

"Her job transferred her to Carson City. She lives in the country, southwest of town."

Bart sank into the armchair he'd been sitting in earlier. "Maybe the BLM will ship her out of here soon," he said sarcastically.

"Dad, that's enough," Orin scolded. "If you

don't have anything better than that to say, then go upstairs and sulk by yourself."

Bart scowled at his son. "Why should I pretend and make nice? I don't like anyone who's hurt my family. Period." He turned his attention to Clancy. "I've heard enough about that woman. Tell me about the land. What did you think?"

Clancy had learned long ago to let Bart's comments roll off him like raindrops on an oiled duster. Otherwise, he would've left this ranch years ago. "It's mostly mountain land with lots of pine," he told his grandfather. "We did find some grazing areas, though, and water."

The mere word pricked both men's ears.

"Water?" Orin repeated. "Everyone has been having hell finding enough water these past few months. I never expected any mountain streams to be running."

"The streams we found were mostly dry rock. This was a little lake or pond—whatever you want to call it. Olivia believes it's fed by a spring. Anyway, someone dammed it years ago and now there's plenty of water for cattle or whatever."

Excited by this news, Bart slapped his thigh. "Well, I'll be damned. I haven't been up that way in years. I thought I was buying desert hill property."

Orin glanced curiously over at his father. "Who owned the place before you?"

"Don't remember the name," Bart said. "Some syndicate back east. I doubt anyone from the group ever looked at the land. They dumped it for a cheap price."

Rising to his feet, Clancy carried his empty mug over to the bar that stretched across one corner of the room. "Well, apparently they didn't bother to look at a geology report, either. Someone used to have a mine up there. Olivia and I found the opening and part of an old flume."

Orin let out a mocking grunt. "That wouldn't be the first one to be found on Horn land. We've probably filled in ten or fifteen of those things over the years. The poor soul probably never made a dime from the thing or if he did, someone knocked him in the head and stole it all. I'll talk to Rafe about getting the men to cover the entrance. Just to make sure it can't crash in on humans or animals."

Ignoring Orin's comments, Bart thoughtfully stroked his chin with a thumb and forefinger. "The mine might have been lucrative at one time, but now I'd say the water is much more valuable to us than ore."

"I'm glad to hear you say that, Dad. While the men are up there blocking up the hole, they can also check on the fence lines. We might put a few steers up there next spring or maybe even some mama cows. You think there'd be enough grass for fifty head?"

The last question was directed at Clancy and

he glanced over at his father. "I'd say so. But Rafe could give you a better idea about that than me."

"What makes you think I might not be interested in the mine?" Bart asked his son. "The thing might have a vein of gold."

Orin snorted. "Gold, hell. You'd probably spend thousands and find nothing."

Bart frowned. "You're forgetting that Nevada still produces eighty percent of the gold found in the United States."

"Not on the Horn," Orin countered. "You've never wanted that before. It would ravage that piece of land!"

Not wanting to get in the middle of an argument, Clancy said, "You two talk it over. I'm going to the kitchen and grab something to eat."

Clancy was stepping into the hallway when his father caught up to him.

"Clancy, just a moment."

Turning, he looked questioningly at Orin. "Is anything wrong, Dad?"

"No. Not at all. I just wanted to—" Pausing, he grimaced, then used his head to motion toward the family room. "Your grandfather and all that stuff about Olivia. Don't pay any attention to him. He's just blowing— The only thing he knows about Olivia is that she hurt you."

Clancy's gaze dropped to a spot on the floor. "You don't have to explain Grandfather's behavior to me."

"It's none of his business. But that's just his way of wanting to protect you."

With a mocking grunt, Clancy lifted his gaze back to his father's face. "Grandfather could be right. I probably do need protecting from Olivia."

Orin frowned. "Why do you say that?"

Shrugging, Clancy let out a long breath. He'd not wanted to get into this sort of discussion about Olivia tonight. But he should've guessed that letting his family know she was living close by would be enough to stir up questions.

"Because I still have feelings for the woman."

Orin was quiet for a long moment and Clancy wondered if his father's silence was a sign of worry or if he was simply trying to carefully choose his next words.

"What sort of feelings?" he finally asked. "Are you saying you still love her?"

Love. Clancy had once believed he loved Olivia. But as the years without her had passed, those feelings had gotten all mixed up with regret and resentment and too many erotic memories. Now the more he tried to detangle them, the more he wondered if he was walking down a dead-end street.

"No. It's not love, Dad. But it's enough to make me want to spend time with her. And I have no idea where that may lead."

"Where do you want it to lead?"

On that mountain meadow, in a house built

for her and their children? The mere idea of it warmed the empty holes in his heart. But it also scared the hell out of him. Even if he was brave enough to make her his wife, how could he ever truly trust her to stay at his side?

Not wanting Orin to see the torn look in his eyes, Clancy glanced to a spot down the hallway. "That's the problem, Dad. I honestly don't know."

With gentle understanding, Orin patted his shoulder. "You'll figure it out, son."

"Yeah, sooner or later."

Orin gave his shoulder one more encouraging squeeze, then stepped back into the family room to rejoin his father.

Clancy walked on to the kitchen, where Greta made an issue of serving him a plate of heated food with a tall glass of iced tea. The meat and accompanying vegetables were delicious, and normally he was a hearty eater, but tonight he could've been eating a pile of hay and not known the difference.

Every cell in his brain was still stuck on that kiss he and Olivia had shared in front of the old mine.

She'd tasted sweet and sultry, and the movement of her soft lips against his had infused him with a desire that was still burning deep within him. He wanted her now just as much as he'd wanted her ten years ago.

His father had said he would figure it all out. Now Clancy could only hope and pray that his father was right.

Chapter Six

A week later, on Sunday morning, Olivia went to church with her neighbor Ezra, then invited him to join her for dinner at her house. As he sat across the table from her and dug into the food with obvious pleasure, she could only wonder why she couldn't have been blessed with a man like him for a father. Instead, when Olivia had been little more than five years old, Chuck Parsons had decided he wasn't a family man and had left their home in Idaho Falls once and for all.

Over time, Olivia had told herself that her father's leaving hadn't really affected her life. After all, she'd had a loving mother who'd worked tirelessly to provide a decent life for Olivia and her brother. She'd not needed a father around, who considered having a job akin to having the measles and a couple of kids to care for about as important as carrying the trash out to the curb. No, Chuck Parsons had been worthless, yet if she searched deep within herself, she'd have to admit he'd skewed her image of men somewhat.

"Normally, I don't even like chicken, but this is delicious, Livvy. What did you do to it?"

Olivia smiled at the older man as he happily bit into a dinner roll. In spite of eating anything and everything he wanted, Ezra was lean and as strong as an ox. No doubt his physical fitness came from the outdoor work of caring for his cattle and the thousand-acre spread he owned. At one time he'd had red hair, but the thick waves were now a motley mix of auburn, copper and gray. His blue eyes were still bright and full of life and though his face was somewhat wrinkled, he was still an attractive man for his age.

"Sprinkled it with spices and herbs and shoved it in the oven," she answered his question. "You can do it. I'll write it down for you."

He chuckled. "It's easier to let you do it. But I can fix a damned good brisket. I'll do that soon and have you over at my place."

"I'd like that," she told him. "And thanks for taking me to church this morning. I really enjoyed it."

A slight grin crossed his weathered face. "Well, I think Dusty Marshall enjoyed it more."

Frowning at the subtle twinkling in his eyes, her fork paused in midair. "Dusty Marshall? Was that the tall, dark-haired guy you introduced me to before the service started?"

"Uh-huh. That's him. He was casting you all sorts of looks throughout the service."

Shaking her finger at him, Olivia scolded, "Ezra, you might as well have stayed home this morning. You were supposed to be listening to the minister, not people watching."

His grin turned sheepish. "You should tell that to Dusty, too. He had his mind on you instead of the sermon."

Olivia rolled her eyes. "I seriously doubt that. And even if he did, he's wasting his time. And you are, too, if you think you're going to hook me up with a man."

Ezra forked another piece of chicken from a platter in the middle of the table. "I've got plenty of time and patience."

Sighing, she reached for her water glass. "Ezra, I've told you that I'm already seeing someone."

He batted a dismissive hand through the air. "Bah. If he was that important, he'd be sitting here at your table instead of me."

Olivia could feel her cheeks turning pink. She and Clancy had made the trip to Bart's mountain property a week ago yesterday and she'd not seen or heard from him since. A fact that confused and disappointed her. Especially since they'd ended the day on warm and friendly terms.

"Maybe you're right." Hoping Ezra couldn't read her expression, she reached for her water glass. "I'm beginning to think I might have read too much into things—with him."

"You've only lived around here for about six weeks. You couldn't have known this fella for very long. Could be he's not all that you believed him to be."

Sighing, Olivia leaned back in her chair. "I've known Clancy for several years. Once upon a time we were—uh—engaged."

Ezra's head jerked up. "Engaged! But you told me that you'd never lived around here before."

"I hadn't. I met Clancy in Las Vegas when we

were in college. He's one of the Calhouns. The family owns the Silver Horn ranch."

The older man's jaw dropped, a reaction that Olivia often witnessed from people when the Calhoun name was mentioned. It was a constant reminder that the family was regarded as ranching royalty in this part of the state.

He whistled under his breath. "You were going to marry one of the Calhouns? What happened?"

Shrugging, she dropped her gaze to the food on her plate. "We were young and family issues happened."

Ezra snorted. "Guess this Clancy's parents thought he could do better or something like that. Rich folks have a different mind-set as to what's important. They think money is the center of the universe, where me and you think it's love."

Smiling now, she looked across the table at him. "You old softie, your wife must have adored you."

His grin was rueful. "She had to work at it at times. But she hung with me for thirty-seven years. I like to think if she hadn't died, she'd still be with me today."

"There's no question of that," Olivia said, then rising to her feet, she went over to the cabinet counter, switched on the coffeemaker and gathered two cups from a nearby shelf. "I should tell you, though, that the family issue with me and Clancy wasn't his family, but mine. I had to leave college and care for my mother. She'd been diagnosed with cancer and after that I couldn't make many future plans. Since I was the only caretaker she had, that kept me pretty tied down. Everything was uncertain at that time in my life. I didn't have much choice but to end things with Clancy. He didn't take it well. I think—well, a part of him still hates me for leaving him."

Ezra was silent for so long that Olivia glanced over her shoulder to see he was regarding her thoughtfully.

"Pride," he said. "We men have a lot of it. And sometimes it's hard for us to set it aside."

Olivia nodded that she understood what Ezra was trying to say, then turned back to the coffeemaker. After a moment, she heard his footsteps behind her and turned to see he'd left the table to join her at the cabinet counter.

"You've told me that your mom died. It would be nice if you had her around now to give you advice. What about your dad? Where does he live?"

Olivia let out a caustic laugh. "God only knows. I've not seen him in several years and that was not much more than a brief hello. You see, when I was just a little girl, he deserted us."

Once Olivia had met Ezra it hadn't taken her long to figure out the man had a soft heart and she could see it now as his blue eyes misted over.

"Aw, that's a shame."

Turning back to the countertop, Olivia filled

two cups with the strong brew. "Don't feel bad for me, Ezra. I don't need him."

"Is that right? I thought all little girls needed their daddy."

Steeling herself against the cold emptiness of that thought, she slowly stirred cream into one of the coffees. "I learned not to need mine."

Long moments passed before he finally asked, "So your mom never remarried?"

Turning back to him, she handed him the coffee. "No. Chuck Parsons cured her of wanting another husband."

"Oh. Must have been a swell guy," he said sarcastically.

"Yeah. Swell." She motioned for him to return to the table. "You go sit and I'll bring you dessert."

"Dessert? What is it?"

She cast a playful scowl at him. "Does it matter?"

"Okay. I'll go sit." Chuckling, he started in

the direction of the table, then suddenly paused and turned back. "Livvy, I never had a daughter. Just one boy and he lives in another state now. If you ever decide you need a stand-in daddy, I'll be around."

Blinking at the moisture rushing to her eyes, she gave him a grateful smile. "Thank you, Ezra."

Later that evening, Clancy muttered a curse under his breath and tossed the cell phone onto the passenger seat as he drove down the black-topped country road that led to Olivia's house. Since his plane had landed at the airport a little more than thirty minutes ago, he'd rung her number three times, but she'd yet to answer.

And maybe she didn't want to, he thought. He'd let a week pass without contacting her. A week that had been filled with long meetings and longer dinners with cattlemen that wanted to talk about modern ranching. Clancy had been bored to tears. The Silver Horn worked in the same way of the traditional ranches in Texas. Everything was done on horseback. There were no helicopters swooping down, terrifying herds of mama cows or loud four-wheelers buzzing through the pastures sending steers and heifers racing to the brush for safety.

Clancy had made his case for the old, traditional methods and he'd done his duty making the rounds with business acquaintances, but between it all, his mind had been occupied with Olivia. He'd wanted to call her. He'd wanted to hear her voice. Yet each time he'd picked up the phone all he'd been able to do was stare at her number.

What could he have said to the woman? *I'm here in Las Vegas and all I can do is think about the time we spent here together?* Or *I wish you were here in Las Vegas with me so that we could go to the nearest wedding chapel and do what we should've done ten years ago?*

Hell, he shouldn't have been thinking about any of those things. He should've called and simply explained where he was and that he'd see her soon. But he'd not even been able to do that much. Instead, he'd spent part of the time trying to convince himself that second chances rarely worked and he was stupid to think a second time around with Olivia would turn out any better.

But now, after eight long days without seeing or talking with her, he realized that none of that mattered anymore. To hell with caution. He wanted the woman.

Fifteen minutes later, when Clancy pulled to a stop in front of Olivia's house, it was almost dark, but there was still enough light for him to see Olivia in the yard playing fetch with her dogs. She was bundled in a quilted nylon coat and a sock cap pulled snugly over her long hair.

Spotting him, she turned and waved, and with a sense of relief he switched off the engine and left the truck.

"Hello," she called out as she and the dogs met him on the sparse yellow grass of the lawn.

"Hello," he replied.

As she halted a few steps away from him, he noticed her cheeks and nose were a rosy-red from the cold, her eyes squinted against the wind. He was itching to grab her and pull her into his arms. Instead, he jammed his hands in the pockets of his leather jacket.

"I never expected to see you here tonight," she said.

"I only landed at the airport about forty minutes ago. I tried to call three or four times on the way out here, but you didn't answer."

The dogs continued to nudge his legs for attention and as he waited for her to reply, he bent over and gave both animals a few gentle strokes on the head.

"Airport? You've been out of town?" she asked.

Straightening away from the dogs, he answered, "Las Vegas for the past five days. A cattlemen's convention. Dad was supposed to have gone, but he had other obligations, so I was chosen to take his place."

Thoughtful now, she patted the pockets on her coat. "I must have left my phone in the house. I've been here in the yard for close to an hour."

He couldn't stop his eyes from roaming to the top of her head, down to the toes of her cowboy boots. Even in old work jeans and her face bare of makeup, she looked sexier than any woman he'd ever seen.

"Well, I thought I'd take a chance and drive by your place before I went home."

Hell, who was he trying to fool? She knew he'd driven fifteen miles off the beaten path to get here. And with no more than a hope that she'd be home.

"I see. Well, what about all last week? Your phone wasn't working?"

Knowing he probably looked guilty as heck,

he reached for her arm and turned her toward the house. "Let's go in. I don't want to talk out here in the cold. Or am I welcome?"

She looked at him and her chilly expression had nothing to do with the winter weather.

"Come on," she muttered. "I'll make us something warm to drink."

Clancy didn't say anything else as he followed her into the house, but after they'd both shed their coats and he'd placed his hat on a wall table, he turned to her. "This probably isn't going to mean much to you, Livvy, but I'm sorry I didn't call."

She stood before him, her eyes drilling into his. "To be honest, Clancy, I hadn't known what to think. I'd pretty much decided I wasn't going to hear from you again," she admitted.

That stunned him. "You actually thought that?"

Scowling, she asked, "Why, wouldn't I? Barring

being in a coma, you could've at least sent me a text."

Folding his arms against his chest, he leveled a pointed look at her. "I haven't exactly been bombarded with calls and texts from you."

Her lips pressed together. "I'm not going to chase after any man. Not even you, Clancy. Call me old-fashioned if you want, but if a man is interested he ought to give a woman a sign. And this past week you've ignored me."

Feeling like a heel and an idiot on top of it, he stepped closer. "I wasn't ignoring you on purpose, Livvy. Things got hectic. But I…"

As his voice awkwardly trailed away, she finished with a note of sarcasm. "But you didn't have time between all those meetings you attended. Right?"

He blew out a frustrated breath. "I'm not going to use that excuse. I had the time. But each time I pulled out the phone I didn't know what I could say."

Her eyes rolling, she turned away from him and walked over to the middle of the living room where the drapes were opened to a view of the starry sky. At the back wall, logs burned in the fireplace and the orange glow of the fire silhouetted the curves of her body and turned her dark hair to the color of burgundy wine. And in spite of her cool greeting, desire stirred in him like a hot, desert wind.

"Clancy, if you didn't know what to say to me then, how could you possibly know what to say now?"

Groaning, he walked over to her, but stopped short of laying his hands on the back of her shoulders. "Go ahead and tell me how stupid that sounds. I won't try to deny it."

When she failed to reply, he stepped in front of her and reached for both her hands. As his fingers tightened around hers, he said, "Livvy, I didn't call you these past few days because I was doing a lot of thinking. About you. About us. And I decided that the next time I spoke to you, I didn't want it to be just small talk."

Her eyes searched his face and as he waited for some sort of response, he realized just how important she'd already become to his life. If she told him she never wanted to see him again, he'd be devastated. It was that simple and that scary.

Oh, Lord, what did that mean? That he was falling in love with her again? Or that he'd never stopped loving her?

The questions were rolling over and over in his mind, when she spoke in a hoarse whisper.

"So—where did all this thinking get you?"

His gaze locked on to hers and suddenly his throat was so tight he wasn't sure he could continue breathing, much less talk.

Moving closer, he tucked her hands against the middle of his chest. "I'm tired of pretending, Livvy. I'm tired of trying to convince myself that we ought to take things slowly. When all I really want to do is this."

He didn't give her enough time to ask what "this" meant. Instead, he circled his arms around her and lowered his face to hers.

As he watched her eyes fill with surprise, she whispered in a choked voice, "I thought you were going to say you wanted to end things with me."

His heart winced at the thought. "Not end, Livvy. I want things to start. Right here. Right now."

She let out a long breath and as her fingers curled into his chest, he wondered if she could feel his heart hammering. Could she feel how very much he wanted her?

"So do it, Clancy. Now. Right this second."

He didn't need to hear more. Closing his hand around her chin, he brought his lips down on hers, and as their softness yielded beneath his, he forgot everything except the warmth of her curves pressing into him, the taste of her mouth and the restless search of her hands against his chest.

* * *

Olivia wasn't thinking. If she had been, she would've never invited him into the house. She would've told him to get lost and go torture some other woman with his hot and cold attitude. But this was Clancy. This was the rancher she'd never been able to forget. And the taste of his lips against hers was like a soothing balm to all the wounds she'd ever suffered in her life.

Eventually, he eased his mouth away from hers, and by then Olivia's senses had flown in all directions. "Clancy, we've wasted so much time," she whispered between gulps of air. "Let's not waste any more."

His tough hands slipped to her face and cradled her cheeks. "Livvy, are you sure? Really sure? The other day on the mountaintop—"

Shaking back her tangled hair, she linked her hands at the back of his neck. "My pride was getting in the way. But pride can get to be a cold thing—especially when I know how special things can be between us."

His gaze searched her face one last time and then with a needy groan, his lips fastened roughly over hers.

This time there was no holding back on her part or his. Their mouths fused with hot hunger and as he crushed her close to his long, lean body she wrapped her arms tightly around his waist and surrendered to the pleasure of being in his embrace.

The sound of the crackling fire mingled with the throbbing heartbeat in her ears, but after a while even those sounds were lost to her. The familiar surroundings of the room fell away, leaving nothing but the anchor of his hard body and the unquenchable desire rushing through her.

When he finally tore his mouth away from hers and they both fought to regain their breaths, Olivia knew there was no turning back for either of them. And she didn't want to turn back. For years she'd longed for and dreamed about being in Clancy's arms again. She didn't want to analyze the right or wrong of it anymore. She didn't want to worry about tomorrow or the next day or a month from now. She had to snatch what happiness this man could bring her at this very moment.

"Let's get on the couch," he said.

"No I have a better suggestion." Wrapping her hand around his, she whispered, "Come with me."

She guided him out of the living room to the end of a short hallway. The door to her bedroom stood open and a shaft of dim light from the window cast slanted shadows across the queen-size bed covered with a rose-pink comforter.

When they reached the side of the mattress, she dropped his hand and turned to switch on a small lamp on the nightstand. The soft glow was just enough to bathe the bed in warm light.

"Do we need the lamp?" he asked.

Turning back to him, she reached for the snaps on his shirt and as the fabric parted beneath her hands, she smiled up at him. "I want to be able to see you. All of you."

The sharp intake of his breath sent a shiver of pleasure through her and she hurried to push the tails of his shirt out of the way so that her palms could wrap against his hard, warm abdomen. Oh, how precious it was to be able to touch him again, she thought. To drink in his scent and press her lips against his heated skin.

"Livvy. Sweet Livvy."

He breathed the nickname against the top of her hair and she turned her face to nuzzle her cheek against his bare chest.

"When I saw you that morning in the Grubstake this is all I could think about," she admitted, her voice hoarse with passion. "It felt like we'd never been apart."

His fingers gently tugged the hair at the back of her head until her face was tilted up to his.

"I wanted to snatch you up in my arms, Livvy. I didn't know how you felt or even if you belonged to another man. I only knew that I wanted you." He crushed her closer as his lips hovered over hers. "This is the way it's meant for us to be."

Her heart swelled with so much longing that she wondered how it could go on beating. "Love me, Clancy," she pleaded.

His lips came down on hers and as his mouth moved slowly and gently against hers, the fire that was already burning low in her belly began climbing higher and higher until heat was sizzling the very top of her head.

By the time the kiss ended, she was desperate to get her hands on him and wasted no time in shoving the shirt off his shoulders, but when she reached for the buckle on his belt, he was quick to grab her hands.

"Let me," he said. "I can do it faster."

"Faster isn't better. Not now," Pulling free of

his hold, she placed a hand on his chest and pushed him backward onto the wide bed, then one by one tugged off his boots and set them aside. By then he grabbed her by the wrist and attempted to pull her onto the bed with him, but she resisted and went to work unbuckling his belt.

Casting him a suggestive smile, she purred, "Patience, cowboy."

"Patience? Livvy, this is torture."

"Hmm. A good kind of torture, though, right?"

His groan was more like a gurgling laugh and she knew desire was already pushing him to the edge, just as it was pushing her to touch him everywhere, to feel his manhood driving deep within her.

"Hurry—Livvy," he urged in a choked voice. "I can't wait. I—"

The rest of his words broke off abruptly as she levered the zipper on his fly downward, then slipped her hand inside his jeans. As her fingers closed around him, he gasped and snatched her wrist.

"It has to be faster, Livvy," he said gruffly. "Or this is going to end before it starts."

Relenting, she eased her hand away and quickly jerked on the hems of his jeans until the denim slipped off his feet. Before they fell to the floor, he was reaching for her and while his hands urgently went to work removing her clothing, she occupied herself with planting kisses along his collarbone and swirling her fingertips through the patch of red-gold hair on his chest.

As soon as he had her naked, he tugged her down beside him on the bed and wrapped a tight arm around her waist.

"You feel incredible," he mouthed against her cheek. "So smooth and soft and warm."

Thrusting her fingers into his tawny hair, she turned her lips toward his. "I've imagined this so many times, Clancy. Too many to count."

"So have I, my darling. So have I."

With his hand low on her back, he drew her hips toward him and the feel of his arousal pressed against her belly left her frantic with desire.

She threw her leg over his and he eased his head back to look at her.

"Do you have some sort of birth control?" he asked in a husky rush. "Because I'm not carrying anything with me."

"Don't worry. I'm protected. The Pill."

Relief flashed in his eyes and words became unimportant as he rolled her over onto her back and crushed his mouth over hers.

With his lips feasting on hers, his hands began exploring, reacquainting themselves with the curves and contours of her body. Each stroke of his fingers burned and branded and staked the territory as their own and Olivia was consumed with the urge to somehow give him more. Not just more of her body, but also the deepest part of her very soul.

By the time his mouth finally deserted hers and his tongue started a wet descent down the tender slope of her neck, she was making mewing little sounds in her throat, while her hands attempted to clutch him even closer.

Twisting and turning, she writhed beneath him as eagerness and need engulfed her like a giant wave. The exhilaration was practically suffocating and yet it wasn't enough. She wanted more from him, even if it meant she'd never draw another breath.

Clutching his hips, she gasped. "You're torturing me now, Clancy. And we've waited too long. Much too long."

"Oh, baby—way too long."

His words were riding on a guttural groan and she recognized that he was as equally lost in this moment as she, that he was on the same driven path that she was racing down.

Lifting himself up, he braced a hand on either side of her head and she unconsciously opened her thighs and invited him to make that last ultimate connection with her.

He didn't hesitate and as he slowly entered her, the overwhelming shock of having him inside her caused her eyes to glaze with moisture and her teeth to snap together.

It wasn't until he'd sunk himself completely into her and begun to move that she felt herself breathe again, and by then the fire that was searing her lungs had spread to every cell of her body.

His driving thrusts were pushing and pulling her to a mystical garden where the dark sky above them was filled with millions of twinkling stars and the sound of their breathing was lost among the musky leaves and tangled branches.

Straining to match the rhythm of his movements, she clung to his sweaty back and paced her hips with his, but the pace soon became so frenetic she lost all control. Awareness blurred to little more than flashes of color and slices of pleasure so intense it was very close to pain.

Sensing that she was on the verge of spinning away, she gripped his shoulders and cried his name. He instantly covered her mouth with his and she arched desperately toward his hard body. His hands gripped her hips and as he ground into her with one final plunge, she felt her heart splitting, bursting with emotions she couldn't hold back.

Long moments later, after both of them had regained their breaths and the sweat on their skin began to cool, Clancy rolled his weight off her, then tucked her closely against his side.

Olivia reached behind her and pulled a corner of the comforter over them before she pillowed her cheek on his shoulder. As she snuggled next to him, he stroked fingers through her hair and pressed his lips against the crown of her head. "I sure wasn't planning on this tonight."

The incredulous tone in his voice was so comical she wanted to laugh, but the sound came out more like a weary grunt. "I'd even given up on a phone call from you. Now here you are in my bed."

He said, "I didn't want to go to Las Vegas this past week. I argued with my dad about it, but in the end I decided it was an obligation I needed to keep. I'm glad I did."

She tilted her head so that she could see his face. "You are? Why?"

"Because those days away from you opened my eyes. I kept thinking about our time together on the mountain. All that talk we had about taking things slow and cautious—I didn't want any more of that, Livvy. My Lord, after ten years of waiting—that ought to be enough."

Rising up on her elbow, she stroked her fingers alongside his jaw. "That day you talked about being scared to jump back into a relationship with me. Well, I'm just as scared, Clancy. But I've been doing a lot of thinking, too."

His green gaze gently caressed her face. "And what has all that thinking told you?"

"That I didn't want us to end. That it was foolish for me to try to keep you out of my bed. We were lovers once. And we're lovers now. We'll have to grow from that."

Groaning with pleasure, he rolled her onto her back and kissed her swollen lips. "And we will, my darling. Starting tonight."

Olivia wrapped her arms around him and as she surrendered to the desire building inside her once again, she couldn't help but wonder where all this passion was going to take them. It hadn't kept them together ten years ago. How could it possibly keep them together now?

Chapter Seven

Two weeks later, as the end of September arrived, Clancy had driven out to a west range to see how the fence building crew was progressing. Since miles of the cross-section fence was being replaced, the work was going to take months instead of weeks. Especially when the crew had to deal with the rough terrain of the mountain slopes.

Stopping the truck a short distance away from the busy men, Clancy climbed out to the ground. He was jerking on his leather gloves when he heard the sound of horse hooves approaching behind him.

Glancing over his shoulder, he was surprised to see his father riding up on Woody.

Clancy watched his father rein the black horse to a stop and climb to the ground before he lifted a hand in greeting and called out, "Have you noticed it's freezing this morning? A few flakes of snow hit my windshield on the drive out here."

Orin loosened the girth to give the horse a breather before he walked over to join Clancy.

"I hope this early snow holds. We can use all the moisture we can get. Besides, a little cold never hurt me," Orin said with a chuckle. "It doesn't appear to be slowing down these fence builders, either."

"Yes, but they're—" he caught himself, then continued "—trying to finish a job."

Orin chuckled again. "Don't try to fool me, son. You were going to say these guys are much younger than your old dad." He patted Clancy's shoulder. "It's all right. My hide is tough."

"Well, you're not old by any means. But it is mighty cold for you to be out riding this morning. I'll bet Woody tried to buck with you."

"Only a little," Orin said sheepishly. "I was ready for him, though."

Clancy couldn't help but be amazed at the sight of his robust father bundled in the sheep-lined ranchers jacket and a bright red kerchief tied around his throat. Having a girlfriend had taken fifteen years off his appearance and even more off his attitude about life. Two years ago, Orin would have been sitting at his desk, shuffling paperwork and trying to pretend he was happy. Now Orin was back to being a cowboy and truly happy, and Clancy thanked God every day for the change in his father.

Clancy gestured toward the crew of fence builders. "I thought I'd check on their progress."

"What's been built so far looks good, don't you think?"

That was one thing that Clancy always appreciated about his father. He valued his sons' opinions. Not just about ranching matters, but about everything.

"I'm pleased with the work," Clancy answered. "And happy about the cost, too. I had budgeted for a bigger expense. So you might want to think about where you want to put the extra money. Finn wants a new horse walker."

Orin grunted. "Finn always wants something."

"Did you ride all the way out here just to look at the new fence?" Clancy asked.

Orin turned a squinted gaze to the west where the flat range was interrupted by bald hills. "No. I wanted to get a look at the cows in this section. Rafe tells me they look like they're holding their weight, but I want to see for myself. But I've not run across the herd."

"In this wind you'll probably find them in the

draw about a mile west of here," Clancy suggested. "Want me to drive you over there?"

Orin shot him an insulted look. "I do not. You can get back in your heated comfort. I'm going to climb back on Woody."

"Just offering, Dad."

A few moments of silence passed as the two men watched the busy fence crew, then Orin finally said, "I went by your office this morning, but you'd already left. I wanted to talk to you about tomorrow night."

Clancy glanced at him. "Tomorrow night? Don't tell me there's some sort of meeting we need to attend. I'm planning on spending tomorrow night with Olivia."

Orin smiled as though it was a balmy spring morning instead of an unusually cold autumn. "She's the reason I'm bringing this up. I thought you might want to invite her to have dinner with us here at the ranch. It's Evan's birthday. Remember?"

Clancy let out a guilty groan. "Oh, hell, I'd forgotten," he admitted. "I'm glad you reminded me. I'll drive to town and try to find some sort of gift he might like."

Orin said, "I wouldn't worry about that. I don't imagine Evan is expecting gifts. But he would miss you if you weren't at his birthday dinner."

There went the quiet, intimate night he'd planned to spend with Olivia, he thought ruefully. Because there was no way he'd let down his brother.

Trying to hide his disappointment, he said, "I'll be there."

"What about Olivia?"

Clancy glanced away from his father to the men who were stretching rolls of barbed wire. Since Olivia had returned to his life, Clancy felt a bit like that wire. Stretched to the limit and wondering if or when he might break from the tension. Though he didn't understand where his unease was coming from. Olivia had been welcoming him in her arms as though she never wanted to let him go. Right now, he should be the happiest man on earth. Instead, he could only wonder how long things could keep going before Olivia put an end to things.

"I'll see what she thinks about it."

"You don't sound very enthusiastic."

Scuffing the toe of his boot against the cold, hard ground, Clancy said, "Bringing a woman home to meet his family is an important step. I don't want to give the wrong impression to anybody."

Orin dropped Woody's reins and stepped closer to Clancy. "'Wrong impression'? What the hell does that mean? Ever since you've come back from Las Vegas you've been a stranger around the ranch house at night. Am I wrong in thinking she's the reason?"

In spite of the cold wind on his face, Clancy could feel his cheeks turning red. These past two weeks he'd spent every spare moment he could find having sex with Olivia. But he hardly needed to confess that to his father.

"You're not wrong. I've been spending a lot of time with Olivia," he replied. "As much as we can fit in around our work schedules."

"Hmm. But you're not getting serious about her. Is that it?"

"Something like that," Clancy said briskly.

Orin shook his head in disapproving fashion. "I certainly hope you're not taking advantage of the woman, Clancy. That's not the way Dad and I taught you boys to be."

Clancy very nearly laughed, but caught himself as he saw that his father was dead serious about the matter.

"Oh, Dad, things are different than when you and Grandfather were my age. Besides, Olivia is a grown woman. It's not like I've seduced an innocent teenage girl."

His lips clamped into a tight line, Orin hung his thumbs over the belt of his chaps. "Damn it, son, I don't mean physically! I'm talking about taking advantage of her emotionally."

Stunned by his father's comment, Clancy stared at him. "How—why would you think I'd be doing that?"

Orin's frown deepened. "Because I know you, Clancy. You don't let go of anything easily. She broke your engagement and you've never forgotten that. If I thought for one minute that you were leading her on just as a way to get back at her, I'd bust you in the mouth."

Clancy realized he was gaping at his father, but he couldn't help it. Once he and his brothers had grown out of their teenage years, Orin never interfered with their personal lives. At least, not where women were concerned. That made it harder to understand why his father was digging into him now.

"That's pretty low, Dad. How could you think I would deliberately set out to hurt Olivia in such a way? Or any woman, for that matter?"

"So you're telling me that you're not dating Olivia just for kicks?"

"It's not for kicks or revenge or anything along those lines."

"Hmm. Well, in my opinion, I think you're a little mixed-up about Olivia. But that's your business, not mine. I would like you to invite her to dinner, though. We've all met her before. It's not like she'd be dining with total strangers."

Clancy wasn't going to point out to his father that it had been more than ten years since Olivia had stepped foot on the Silver Horn. He didn't want to add fuel to this discussion.

"I'll see what she thinks about the idea," Clancy told him.

Grinning, Orin patted him on the shoulder. "Good. That's all I ask. Now, me and Woody better get going before this weather turns worse. See you later."

As Clancy watched his father mount the black horse, then take off in a long trot across the sage-dotted land, he tried to shove away the confusion swirling inside him.

I think you're a little mixed-up about Olivia.

Damn it! Why would his father say such a thing? He'd only been dating Olivia for a short time. What the hell was Orin expecting from him? To run out and buy Olivia another huge diamond and beg her to marry him? Well, if that's what his father was waiting for, then he was going to be in for a long wait.

With that self-promise, he jerked the brim of his hat down lower on his forehead and went to inspect the new fence work.

Later that afternoon, after spending several hours trekking over government land inhabited by large herds of wild mustangs, Olivia and Wes returned to the field office. Since there had been reports that some of the horses were starving and straying onto private ranch land in search of something to eat, she and Wes had been asked to evaluate the grazing situation.

In the snack room, she gratefully clutched a cup of hot coffee and stuck her feet toward a space heater sitting on the floor in front of her. "I don't think my feet will ever thaw. Or my fingers, for that matter."

"I thought you were accustomed to working out in the cold," Wes said as he stood at the cabinet, brewing himself a hot drink.

"I am. But the wind was brutal today. I shudder to think how the wildlife survives in this."

Olivia's coworker carried his coffee over to the long utility table where she was seated and took a chair a few spaces down from her.

After taking a sip from his cup, he asked, "So are we in agreement that more hay needs to be spread?"

She looked at him and wondered why the big brawny man didn't make her heart flutter the same way that looking at Clancy did. He was a hardworking, genuine guy who would make some woman a caring husband. But Wes couldn't make her forget about Clancy. No man could.

"That's what I'm going to put in my report. Just as soon as I can get my fingers warm enough to be able to type it up."

"Well, I know the budget is tight for the mustang division and they have to be careful to stay within their means. But if this bad weather doesn't break, those horses are going to starve without extra hay."

"Unfortunately, that's the way I see it, too," Olivia said. "It would be nice if some rich folks around here would donate more to the mustangs."

"There are many folks who do. But we need more of them to help. Maybe you could talk the Calhouns into throwing more dollars or a few ton of alfalfa into the pot? They'd never miss it."

"I'm sure they could spare money, I'm not certain about the hay. But I wouldn't put Clancy on the spot like that. If he offered on his own it would be different."

She'd hardly gotten the words out when a knock sounded behind her. She saw Wes look up with surprise and she glanced over her shoulder to see Clancy standing in the open doorway of the snack room.

"Oh, Clancy!" she murmured with surprise.

He stepped into the room. "Am I interrupting?"

"Not at all," Wes assured him. "In fact, we were just talking about you."

Olivia shot her coworker a cutting glance to let him know she didn't appreciate his big mouth, but Wes ignored her.

"Me?" Clancy asked, his gaze switching between Olivia and Wes.

Feeling a faint blush sweep over her face, Olivia answered, "Actually your family was mentioned. One of the wild horse ranges is going to need extra hay this winter. It would be nice if a few donors would step up to the plate."

"But Olivia refused to ask you," Wes spoke up. "I believe she thinks it would be inappropriate to put you on the spot."

More than annoyed with Wes, Olivia glared at him. "Wes! Don't you have something to do? Like type up a report?"

With a lazy grin, Wes rose to his feet and started toward the door. "Sure, I do. Good to see you again, Clancy."

Clancy nodded. "Same here. And don't let me run you off."

"You're not," Wes assured him. "I have plenty of work to do."

Wes left the room and Clancy walked over to where Olivia was sitting in front of the space heater.

"Was he telling it right? You wouldn't ask me to make a donation to the mustang cause?"

Olivia glanced awkwardly away from him. "I wouldn't use our relationship that way."

He studied her for long moments. "I'd like to think you could ask me anything."

That brought her gaze back around to his and she smiled faintly at him. "Not if the question pertains to money." She placed her cup on the tabletop and rose to her feet. "Would you like something to drink?"

"No thanks. I don't have much time. I'm in town to do some shopping for a birthday gift for Evan."

"Oh. How nice. Do you have something in mind?"

"Not a clue. Evan doesn't do much roping or riding. In fact, outside of being a detective for the sheriff's office, he doesn't do much of anything. But I'll find something to give him."

Shaking back her windblown hair, she reached for his hands and curled her fingers tightly around his. "I'm glad you stopped by, Clancy," she said softly. "I've missed you. Are you still coming over tomorrow night?"

"That's what I'm here to talk to you about. The family is having a special birthday dinner for Evan tomorrow night. I can't miss it."

In spite of being disappointed, she smiled at him. "Of course you can't," she said. "Your brother would miss you if you weren't there."

He placed his hand over the top of hers and the warmth of it was like the summer sun. Suddenly the long hours she'd spent in the cold today seemed like a distant memory.

"I'd like for you to join us, Olivia."

Surprised, she studied his face. "Join you? I'm not so sure such a family celebration would be the right time for me to show up."

"Forget about it being Evan's birthday. Would you like to have dinner at the Silver Horn with me?"

Her heart thudded heavily in her chest. She'd not expected him to invite her to his family home again. Actually, these past weeks since they'd started seeing each other, she'd decided he wanted to keep her completely separated from his family and she'd been telling herself it didn't matter. She didn't need to be accepted by Clancy's family in order for her to have a relationship with him. But now the idea lifted her heart. Maybe he was actually starting to care about her in a serious way.

"I would like to have dinner with you at the Silver Horn," she told him. "It's very nice of you to ask."

He appeared surprised by her response, almost as if he'd expected her to turn down the invitation.

"That's good. Dad was hoping you'd come."

She searched his face as she wondered what he was actually thinking. He hardly looked happy. "Really? And what about you?"

"What do you mean?" he asked quietly.

"I get the feeling you'd like for me to decline the offer."

Releasing a long breath, he glanced away from her. "If the idea of having dinner with my family doesn't bother you, then I'm fine with it."

"Fine with it," she repeated dully, then pulled her hand free of his and walked over to the row of cabinets that covered the back wall of the room. "That sounds very enthusiastic."

"What were you expecting? A *yippee* or *hallelujah?*"

His snide question had her twisting her head around in order to look at him. "Forget it, Clancy. I'll give you a reprieve. Thank your dad for the kind invitation, but I have other things to do."

Before he could make a reply, she turned back to the cabinet and pulled a box of raisins from the shelf.

"But that would be a lie," he said.

"No. It wouldn't be a lie at all. Ezra wants me to go with him to the horse sale up at Reno tomorrow night. I begged off because I thought you were coming over. But he's still going and all I have to do is give him a call and tell him I'm available."

He stalked over to her. "Ezra! You'd rather go with him than have dinner with me and my family?"

His nearness vibrated through her and she could think of little more than stepping into his arms and inviting him to kiss her. "I enjoy Ezra's company and he's offered to help me find a horse I can afford."

"Look, Olivia, I can give you a horse. You don't need to go traipsing off with an old man who's only too happy to find some excuse to spend time with you."

Anger caused her to gasp and square around to face him. "How dare you say something like that about my friend! Who the hell do you think you are? You're the one who has one thing on his mind. Here lately, the only place you've offered to take me is to bed. And furthermore, I don't want you to give me a horse. And I wouldn't accept it even if you tried!"

Turning, she shoved the raisins back into the cabinet and shut the door. Behind her, Clancy rested a hand upon the back of her shoulder, but she shrugged it away. He might think he made the sun rise and set in her world. But he didn't. Not by a long shot.

"Okay, I'm sorry, Olivia," he said in a placating voice. "I shouldn't have said any of that about Ezra. I realize he means a lot to you."

"Damn right, he does. So don't go trying to wedge yourself between us."

He was silent for so long that she finally turned to face him. His expression was remorseful and she wondered how they'd gone from him inviting her to dinner to arguing about her neighbor.

Sighing, she bent her head and rubbed fingers against her eyes. "I'm sorry, too, Clancy. I just— it hurts because I can see that you were inviting me to dinner out of obligation. Not because you really want me there." Lifting her head, she dared him to contradict her. "I'm right, aren't I?"

He grimaced. "Not exactly. I do want you there. It's just that—I don't know what my brothers—my family—are going to think. And I didn't want you to get the wrong impression about things."

Dear God, the more he talked the worse it all sounded. And yet, instead of flying off the handle again, she made herself pause and think. So far Clancy had been up-front with her. He hadn't been making any kind of permanent promises to her and she'd not asked for any. She'd allowed him into her bed because she'd wanted him there. She couldn't expect him to act as though she was that same fiancée he'd presented to his family all those years ago. She was a divorcée and both of their lives had changed.

She fixed her gaze on the toes of her cowboy boots. "Look, Clancy, there's no need for you to worry. I'd never get the impression that you're bringing me home to meet the family in the traditional sense. That's already happened. It won't happen again," she said flatly. "And I won't lead your family into thinking that things are serious between us. Because they aren't. Okay? Or should I go ahead and give Ezra a call?"

"Ezra be damned. I'll be over to pick you up around six."

She looked at him and wondered where she found the strength to keep her eyes from misting over.

"All right. I'll be ready."

The next evening, as Clancy drove to Olivia's house, he wondered what was happening to him. Was she changing or was he? Or were both of them headed in a direction he couldn't control?

The idea put a grimace on his face. Yesterday when he'd stopped by her workplace he'd been a little stunned by her reaction to his invitation to dinner. He'd thought she would be pleased. Instead, she'd seemed almost insulted.

Who the hell do you think you are?... Here lately, the only place you've offered to take me is to bed.

The words she'd flung at him still had enough sting to make him wince. Because now that he'd thought about it, he realized she was right. They had spent most of their time together in bed. But that shouldn't be making him feel guilty. There wasn't anything wrong in showing her how much he wanted her. She'd certainly not objected. In fact, she'd seemed to want sex with him as much as he wanted it with her.

I certainly hope you're not taking advantage of the woman, Clancy.

His father's remark had continued to niggle at him. Especially when he added it to everything Olivia had said to him yesterday. Was he taking advantage of Olivia?

Oh, hell, the notion was ridiculous. Just because a man enjoyed a woman's company didn't mean he was obligated to ask her to join him at the altar. Besides, she'd already jilted him once. Was he supposed to give her a chance to do it a second time?

You say you're not taking advantage of her. But you sure as hell don't want to marry her. Exactly what are you doing with the woman, Clancy?

He pushed the annoying voice away as the turn off to Olivia's house appeared a few short yards down the road. Seeing her again would make him forget all the nagging doubts and questions in his mind.

The dogs met him in the yard and followed him onto the porch. After a short knock with no response, he tried the door and after finding it open, stepped inside.

"Olivia? I'm here," he called out as he passed through the small foyer and into the living room.

Cleo, the calico cat who always stayed hidden when he was around, was curled up on the end of the couch, but looked up in terror as she spotted him.

"Well, I finally get to see the ghost cat," Clancy said in a crooning voice. "Hello, pretty girl."

Not impressed with his sweet talk, Cleo arched her back, then leaped off the couch and shot out of the room.

Trying not to take Cleo's rebuff personally, he walked over to the fireplace and was turning his back to the warmth of the flames when the sound of footsteps rapidly tapping their way across the wooden floor had him glancing toward the arched doorway that led to the rest of the house.

When Olivia appeared, the first thing he noticed was the burgundy dress hugging her shapely curves, then the black high heels on her feet and finally the phone jammed to her ear.

Acknowledging Clancy with a little wave, she walked into the room.

"I'm aware of that, Ezra, but you know what I want and what I can afford. I'll pay you extra for the hauling." She paused, then shook her head. "No. I insist. They aren't giving diesel away around here. Now I've got to get off the phone. Send me a text if you see something you like. You do know how to text, don't you?"

The man's answer must've been comical because she laughed, and the warmth and affection he saw on her face made him suddenly realize just how big of a mistake he'd made when he'd spoken against her neighbor. And it would hardly help his cause now to admit he'd actually done it out of jealousy. God help him. Jealous of a seventy-year-old man. That ought to prove to him that Olivia had once again turned him into a fool.

"Okay. Drive carefully and we'll talk tomorrow," she said, then quickly ending the call, she looked at Clancy. "Sorry about that. Ezra is about to leave for Reno."

"So I gathered," he said, "and he's going to bid on a horse for you. If he finds something suitable. I could do that for you, Olivia."

She slanted him a pointed look as though to say "let's not start that again."

"You're a busy man, Clancy. I wouldn't ask you to."

He drew in a long breath and let it out while wondering why he was letting her remark bother him. He should be relieved that she wasn't putting demands on his time or expecting him to make her his priority. That's what every man wanted, wasn't it? A woman who would give him plenty of space.

She reached for her coat lying across the arm of the couch and Clancy stepped over to help her with the garment.

Holding it behind her, she slipped her arms into the sleeves, and as he smoothed the black leather over her shoulders, he breathed in her sweet flowery scent and let his eyes wander over the dark hair falling into a cascade of waves down her back.

"I don't remember you being so independent when we were in college," he commented.

She turned just enough to give him a rueful smile. "I was young and immature then. Later I learned to take care of myself and my mother. There was no one else but us two. Then after she died and I married Mark, I made the mistake of believing him when he promised to take care of me. After he let me down I swore I'd never depend on a man for anything. And I haven't."

He frowned. "Do you think it's right to lump all men together?"

"No. But I know what's best for me." Smiling at him as though to soften her blunt statement, she buttoned the coat at her throat. "I'm ready. We'd better be going, don't you think?"

"Not before this." Bending his head, he placed

his lips on hers and was immediately relieved to feel her lips cling hungrily to his.

Long moments ticked away before he could make himself lift his head, and even then a big part of him wanted to kiss her again, to lift her into his arms and carry her to bed. At least there he didn't have to think about demands, obligations or the future. In Olivia's arms he forgot everything.

"Too bad we can't stay here tonight," he murmured, his voice husky with desire.

She turned away from him and gathered up her purse lying on a nearby wall table. "Your brother would be disappointed. And so would I."

She started toward the foyer, but before she had a chance to reach the door, he quickly caught up to her and pulled her into his arms.

Her head tilted back and her gray eyes were full of questions as they roamed his face. "What is this about? Have you changed your mind about taking me to the Silver Horn?"

He groaned. "Livvy, I don't know why but everything I say seems to come out wrong."

Her gaze continued to delve into his. "You shouldn't think that. You're only saying what you're feeling."

Frustrated, he said, "I don't think you understand what I'm feeling at all."

She eased back from him. "Then maybe you'd better explain."

"All right, I'm not going to lie. Staying here and making love to you would be a heck of a lot nicer than having dinner with my family. But I do want you to see them again. I think they're all a little curious about the two of us getting together after all these years."

"Hmm. I figure they all resent me for breaking our engagement." She shook her head. "On second thought, they were probably relieved that you weren't going to marry a woman like me. You've never told me how your family reacted."

"A woman like you? What does that mean?"

"Royalty marrying a commoner. That's what it means."

"Oh, hell, I never thought that. My family never thought it. And as for how they felt about us breaking up, I guess they all had different ideas about it. None of them blamed you for going to your mother's side while she was ill, but they couldn't understand you shutting me out."

He didn't add that Bart had clearly disapproved of the idea of his grandson getting back together with the woman who'd jilted him. But since then, Bart had promised Clancy to keep an open mind about Olivia and to treat her civilly if she visited the ranch. Clancy could only hope that his grandfather would be on his best behavior tonight. He wasn't sure the tenuous bond between Olivia and himself was strong enough to bear up to one of Bart's outbursts.

He watched her gaze fall to the front of his shirt.

"That would be impossible to explain to you—

to them," she said lowly. "It wasn't the way I wanted things to be. It was something that I believed would be best for you and for me."

Before this moment it would have made him angry to hear her say such a thing. For all these years, he'd considered her decision to cut him out of her life as wrong. Period. No excuses. But tonight he felt no anger. He could hear something in her voice that couldn't be faked. She'd been hurt by the decisions she'd had to make back then and she was still hurting over them now. And more than anything, he wanted to know the reasons that had pushed her to end their relationship. Otherwise, he couldn't see himself trusting her to stick around in the future.

"Someday soon I hope to understand, Livvy. But right now we'd better be on our way. The family will be waiting."

The faint smile on her face was tinged with regret. "I'll never know what that is like."

Pushing away the urge to tug her into his arms and promise her anything, he wrapped his hand around her elbow and guided her out the door.

Chapter Eight

Compared to the rest of the Silver Horn three-story ranch house, the dining room was a small, cozy room with a wall of windows on one side and a massive wooden buffet and china cabinet against the other. A long oak table filled the center of the room, and tonight it was decorated festively with bowls of yellow and copper mums alternated with fat white flickering candles.

As everyone around the table enjoyed the main course of prime rib, Olivia decided the room looked almost as it had ten years ago when she'd visited Clancy's home for the first and only time. As for his family, they'd not changed in appearance much, either, except that Orin had a bit more gray hair and Bart a few more wrinkles.

Clancy's brothers, Evan, Rafe and Finn, had all matured into handsome, rugged men with red-haired Finn looking more like Clancy and Evan and Rafe favoring their late mother, Claudia. Bowie, the youngest of the brothers, had been expected to return home more than two years ago from a long stint in the marines, but at the last minute he'd decided to reenlist. From what Clancy had told her, Bowie's decision had greatly disappointed his father and grandfather. Even so, it was evident to Olivia that the mention of Bowie's name always elicited proud comments from the whole family.

Though it was male dominated, there were a few women—Rafe's wife, Lilly, was there with their baby daughter, Colleen, and the mysterious half sister, Sassy, with her husband and son, along with Orin's date, Noreen. The kids had been fed earlier and were put down to sleep.

"So tell us, Olivia, is your work much different here in Nevada than it was in southern Idaho?" Orin asked.

Feeling as though every eye in the room was on her, Olivia glanced toward the end of the table where Orin was seated. He and everyone in the family had been warm and welcoming to her. But then, she'd not expected anything less from Clancy's family. They were not only a classy bunch, but they loved and respected Clancy too much to treat her with anything less than kindness.

"The terrain is different somewhat and so is the weather. And I've never seen so many old abandoned mines on the land around here," she said.

Bart spoke between bites of rare beef. "Clancy told us about the old mine you two found on the

Rock Mountain range. I've been wanting to go up there and take a look at it myself. What do you think, Olivia? Think there might be any valuable ore there?"

The unexpected question caused her to pause, while down the table Orin frowned at his father.

"Dad, what kind of question is that? We're going to send a dozer up there to close off the entrance of the cave."

Bart leveled a pointed look at his son. "I never said anything about filling the mine in. You did. And the last time I looked, I still run this place," he told Orin, then focused his attention back on Olivia. "Now that we have that out of the way, what's your opinion?"

Glancing quickly at Clancy, she could see a bit of an anxious look on his face. As though he half expected an argument to ensue. '

Deciding the only thing she could do was give her honest opinion, she said, "Well, actually, sir, minerals aren't my forte. A geologist is what you need to give you that answer. But one thing was obvious to me. A long time ago, someone up on that mountain had a dream. The real mystery is whether he found it or not."

The eldest Calhoun studied her for long moments, then lifted his wineglass and nodded in her direction. "Well said, Olivia. Oftentimes a man's dreams are more important than what he can grasp with his hands. Without them life would be mundane." Bart looked across the table at Evan, the birthday honoree. "I hope you hold on to all your dreams, son. And may they all come true."

Everyone around the table lifted their glasses to join Bart's toast.

"To Evan," Orin added with obvious affection for his middle son, "may you have a long and happy life."

"And find a nice woman to put up with you, too," Finn tacked on. "Before you get too old to enjoy one."

Finn's wish for his brother brought a good-natured groan from Evan and chuckles among the others around the table.

Clancy was seated immediately to Olivia's left and as she returned her glass to the tabletop and picked up her fork, she felt his gaze upon her. Glancing over at him, she saw him studying her with a look on his face she'd never seen before.

"Is anything wrong?" she asked.

"No. You're looking especially beautiful tonight. That's all."

She gave him a coy smile. "Keep drinking that wine. It seems to be working."

Beneath the table he reached for her hand and for one brief moment as he squeezed her fingers, Olivia let herself imagine how things would have been if her mother hadn't become ill, if she'd not left college and Clancy's side. Would she be sitting here as his wife? As a member of this family?

While they finished the remainder of the meal,

she tried not to allow her thoughts to dwell on the past. It couldn't be undone. She had to focus on the future and try to figure out if Clancy was going to remain a part of it.

After dinner everyone retired to the family room located at the back of the house. Tessa served coffee, and as Olivia stood near the fireplace, sipping her cream-diluted brew, Finn emerged from one of the groups where Clancy was deep in conversation and walked over to join her.

"Would you like anything else, Olivia? More coffee or birthday cake?" he offered.

Groaning with contentment, she patted her flat stomach. "I hardly have room for the rest of this coffee. Everything was delicious."

He smiled at her and Olivia couldn't help thinking how much more open this man was than Clancy. Letting his thoughts and opinions fly out in the open seemed to be especially easy for Finn. But Clancy had never been one to lay out his feelings on matters unless he was pushed to do so. Mostly he kept his feelings hidden behind a dark, closed wall. A wall that Olivia had tried to knock down, but failed.

"So are you enjoying yourself?" Finn asked. "There are so many of us we can be a bit overwhelming at times."

With a slight shake of her head, Olivia said, "It's nice to see your big family together. I only have one brother. But he's been MIA since I was a teenager."

"He's military as well, like Bowie?"

She grimaced. "He was in the army a long time ago. But not anymore. I just meant that Todd has never been family oriented. I don't even know where he lives now."

"Oh. I can't imagine that. What about your father? Is he still living?"

Clearly, Clancy had not discussed her family or lack of one with his brothers, and that told her much about their relationship. He didn't consider her important enough to talk about with his family. Or he was too embarrassed to tell them about the dysfunctional home she'd come from. "The last I heard he was still alive. But it's hard to know since I've only seen him twice in the past ten years."

Finn's expression turned sheepish. "Sorry, Olivia. Everyone tells me I talk too much. I sure put my foot in my mouth this time. But I didn't know about your family."

"No. I don't suppose Clancy has mentioned me that much."

The redheaded Calhoun grimaced. "Clancy doesn't mention much of anything. Period. Getting information out of him is like digging a cactus spine out of your finger. The more you dig, the deeper it burrows under your hide."

"Yes," Olivia agreed. "I do know that about him."

Finn shrugged. "He's all business, you know.

He thinks fun is studying the cattle market report."

Laughing softly, Olivia asked, "And what do you consider fun, Finn?"

He grinned. "Going out with a pretty girl. Like you. Course, seeing a foal born is mighty fun, too." Sipping his coffee, he turned his gaze to a spot across the room where Clancy and Rafe were in deep discussion. "Clancy tells me you're a champion for the wild horses and burros."

Surprised, she stared at Finn. Maybe she'd been wrong in thinking Clancy didn't want to talk about her to his family. The notion made her wonder if she'd assumed other things about him that weren't entirely right.

She said, "Well, I suppose I am. In a round-about way. My coworker and I have been evaluating the grazing conditions on a particular range near here. We'd like to see more hay spread this winter. Otherwise it's going to be tough for some of the horses to survive."

"The Silver Horn donates to the cause every year," he said. "But I'd like to give you a personal check of my own before you leave this evening."

"Oh. That's awfully nice of you. But I'm not here to solicit funds for the Wild Horse and Burro Program."

He shook his head. "Believe me, Olivia, you're not twisting my arm. From the time I was a little boy I've had a fascination for mustangs. And since I've become the manager of the horse division here on the ranch, I've been thinking more and more about incorporating some of the mustang breeding into our working remuda. I happen to believe it would make the foundation of our horse breeding much stronger."

Surprised that Finn had this serious side to him, she said, "That's very interesting. I understand they're usually strong boned and full of stamina. I can see how they'd make useful working horses."

He slanted her an appreciative grin. "Too bad my dad and grandfather can't see it that way. I'm still arguing my cause."

Smiling back at him, she said, "I have a feeling you're a very persuasive man. Don't give up."

Finn was about to make some sort of reply, but at that moment, Sassy, their half sister, walked up to the two of them. She was a tall, lovely young woman with bright blue eyes and rich red hair that waved all the way down her back to her waist. She looked incredibly like Finn, and throughout the evening Olivia had noticed that the two siblings appeared to be extra close.

"Olivia, I know Finn's company is hard to resist, but now that Clancy has finally left your side for a few minutes, Lilly and I thought you might like to join us upstairs to visit the babies."

Although she'd not yet seen the children, Olivia had learned that Rafe and Lilly had a baby daughter while Sassy and Jett had a tod-dler son.

"I'd love to see them," she told Sassy.

"Babies," Finn teased. "I'd say they're more like two little monsters."

Rolling her eyes at him, she patted her lower belly. "And don't forget that another is on the way."

"Poor Jett," Finn continued to joke. "What has the man gotten himself into?"

"We need more ranch hands so Jett's decided we should raise them ourselves." Winking at Olivia, she motioned for her to join her. "C'mon before I bop my brother over the head."

She followed Sassy out of the family room, then on to a long staircase. As they climbed to the second floor, Olivia said, "I wasn't aware that you and your husband were expecting. Congratulations."

"Thanks. I'm almost into my fourth month, so I feel pretty confident about telling people now."

"How old is your son?" Olivia asked.

"Sixteen months. And I'm already convinced he's going to break an Olympic record in the hundred-meter dash. I can't keep up with him."

By now they'd reached the second-floor landing and Sassy glanced curiously over at her. "Would you like to have children, Olivia?"

It was an innocent enough question, but it still had the power to hurt. Yet Olivia did her best to answer as casually as she could. "I've always wanted children. But after my marriage didn't work out, I realized more than ever that I needed the right man in my life to start a family with. Unfortunately, that man hasn't come along yet."

Sassy's expression was full of understanding. "Well, you still have time to find the right man and have babies," she suggested.

The right man had been in her life once, she thought wistfully. She and Clancy had even talked about the children they'd hoped to have after they were married. But she'd given him up and now he didn't want to marry or have children with her, Olivia could've told Sassy. But she wasn't going to reveal such a personal thing to Clancy's sister. He wouldn't appreciate it. And frankly, Olivia wasn't ready to admit to herself, or anyone, that Clancy only considered her a temporary lover.

"Yes. Maybe later...with the right man."

At the top of the landing, Olivia followed her to a spacious bedroom where Lilly was sitting on the floor with a little boy that clearly belonged to Sassy. The toddler possessed the same bright red hair as his mother.

As they entered the room, Rafe's wife smiled at them. "I see you rescued her from the den of lions. Come on over and take a look at my little nephew," she told Olivia.

The child was busy playing with a stack of farm animals, but as Olivia and Sassy approached, he looked up at the two of them, then thrust a black-and-white cow toward his mother and squealed with joy.

Bending over her son, Sassy took the cow and placed it in a tiny trailer sitting close to Lilly's knee. "Now Bessie the cow is all ready to take to the ranch. See if you can drive the truck," she told him, then straightening, she said to Sassy, "As if you hadn't already guessed, this is J.J. Short for Joshua Jett."

Olivia smiled down at the impish little boy dressed in jeans and a cowboy shirt. He'd followed his mother's suggestion and was now pushing the truck and trailer across the hardwood floor.

"He looks so much like you. And Finn," she remarked.

Sassy chuckled. "Yes, Uncle Finn thinks J.J. is just about it."

And what about Clancy? Olivia wondered. Did he look at these children and ever want any of his own? And what if he did? What, then?

Would he ever want to make a family with her? She doubted it. Having children together meant loving and trusting your partner. And so far Clancy wasn't showing her either of those things.

Olivia watched the sturdy little boy at play for a few more moments before she glanced around the room. "Where is your little girl, Lilly?"

Her smile full of affection, Rafe's wife pointed to a crib in the corner of the room. "Colleen is asleep, for now. Go take a look at her. And don't worry about making too much noise. A marching band would have trouble waking her."

Olivia walked over to the crib and stared down at the slumbering child. The baby was lying on her back, a pink blanket pulled up to her shoulders and a little white bow was attached to the wavy wisps of blond hair atop her head. She was as equally adorable as J.J., and as Olivia studied the girl's rosy smooth cheek and tiny clenched fist her heart winced with regret.

Ten years ago, having children of his own had been important to Clancy and something he'd talked a lot about. Becoming parents together had been one of their shared dreams. But the long years apart had apparently buried those dreams. Now he didn't talk about being a father or having babies in his life. Nor did he ever mention becoming a husband. And she was beginning to doubt he ever would.

The dejecting thoughts were still going through Olivia's head when Sassy joined her at the side of the crib.

"She's a gorgeous little doll, isn't she?" Sassy asked, clearly fond of her niece.

Bands of regret were restricting her throat, forcing Olivia to swallow before she replied, "She certainly is. How old is she?"

"Three months."

"She's precious and so is your son," Olivia murmured, then glanced over at Sassy. "Are you wanting a daughter this time?"

"Jett is. To me it doesn't matter."

Sassy turned and walked across the room to take a seat on the edge of the big king-size bed. Olivia took one last look at the precious baby before she walked over to take a seat a short space away from Sassy.

"I hear you're an outdoor girl," Olivia said to her. "So am I."

Nodding, Sassy smiled. "I've heard the same thing about you. Your job sounds very interesting."

"It is," Olivia agreed. "But it's not quite like being a mother. You two ladies are very blessed."

With J.J. happily occupied with his plastic animals, Lilly rose from the floor and took a seat in a stuffed chair positioned near the head of the bed.

"So how are things going with you and Clancy?" Lilly asked frankly.

Sassy gasped. "Lilly! I can't believe you asked her that! I'm the one who's always asking nosy questions."

The blonde, who worked as a nurse in a medical clinic in town, was petite and pretty, and Olivia hadn't missed the loving gazes Rafe had tossed at his wife throughout dinner. They'd been entirely different from the sultry gazes Clancy gave Olivia. Rafe's exchanges with his wife had been tender and reverent, whereas the glances Clancy tossed at Olivia were nothing but hot and sexual.

"I guess you've been rubbing off on me," Lilly told Sassy with a chuckle, then looked at Olivia. "I'm sorry. You don't have to answer that question. But to be honest, the whole family is wondering. Clancy never was one to talk much—especially about his personal feelings."

Olivia felt her cheeks growing warm. "There's not much I can tell you. Other than we like spending time together. And I think this second time around both of us want to be—cautious." She shook her head. "Actually, I was surprised to even be invited to Evan's party. I expected everyone to be—well, resentful of me."

Lilly and Sassy exchanged rueful glances.

"I'm sorry you felt that way," Lilly said.

"I'd like to know how in the world you found the courage to come tonight?" Sassy asked.

Olivia shrugged. "If I plan to be a part of Clancy's life I can't very well hide from his family."

"Well, as far as Lilly and I are concerned, we're hoping you and Clancy are headed toward the marriage altar," Sassy said frankly. "The man needs a wife and we think you're perfect for him."

Tears suddenly stung Olivia's eyes and when she spoke her voice was husky with emotion, "I never thought you two would feel that way about me. Clancy did once. But I doubt he ever will feel that way again."

Sassy scooted down the side of the bed until she reached Olivia's side, then wrapped a comforting arm around her shoulders. "Listen, Olivia, we know all about you breaking the engagement because your mother was terminally ill. You were put in a terrible situation and Clancy should've understood that you didn't have a choice in the matter."

"Actually, I think the whole situation is Clancy's fault," Lilly put in. "He should have gone to Olivia's side and helped her and her mother in any and every way he could."

Olivia had never discussed her breakup with Clancy with anyone. Even her own mother. When she'd gone back to Idaho without Clancy's ring on her finger, she'd simply explained to Arlene that she and Clancy had come to the mutual agreement that they weren't ready to be engaged. And thankfully Arlene hadn't questioned Olivia's explanation. But oftentimes Olivia wondered if her mother had really known what had happened and had been considerate enough not to probe her daughter's private feelings.

Shaking her head, Olivia said, "It wasn't entirely Clancy's fault. I told him not to come. I told him to get on with his life—without me."

"So what? All of us women say things like that," Lilly said. "I'll bet you were wishing and hoping deep down that he would show up on your doorstep and take you in his arms. Isn't that right?"

Oh, God. Lilly was so right it was almost scary. For days and months, even as long as two years after she'd left college and gone back home to Idaho, Olivia had watched and waited and prayed that Clancy had loved her enough to ignore her wishes and plow his way back into her life. But he'd not shown up. He'd not even called once or so much as written a letter. That was enough to convince her that she needed to forget him completely. But he was one rancher she'd not been able to forget.

"Yes. I wanted that desperately." Olivia spoke

in a strained voice. "But he had his own feelings about the matter."

Sassy gave her shoulder another encouraging squeeze. "Look, Olivia, it takes men a whole lot longer to understand things. Sometimes they never do. That's when we women have to sort of help them figure it out on their own."

"Well, that's to say if you think Clancy is worth all that trouble," Lilly added slyly.

He was worth it. But would he ever think she was worthy of being in his life on a permanent basis?

Later that night, as Clancy drove Olivia home, he decided the whole evening with his family had confused him. If anything, he'd expected his brothers to treat Olivia politely, but coolly. After all, his entire family was aware she'd crushed his heart. But it appeared to him that the whole bunch had forgotten that fact. They'd gone out of their way to welcome her. Even his

tough-hided grandfather, who'd merely promised to be polite to Olivia, had turned on the
charm and attempted to make her feel at home.
If a person hadn't known better, he would think
Clancy was the one who'd broken their engagement and Olivia had been the wronged party.

*Well, hell, Clancy, what were you wanting
from your relatives? For them to put her head
on a chopping block? They've clearly forgiven
her. So why can't you?*

The question shooting through his thoughts
came out of the blue and stung him hard. He had
forgiven her, hadn't he? He'd taken her back into
his arms and his bed. Yeah, but he'd not taken
her into his heart, he concluded. And that was
a step he wasn't sure he could ever take.

"I have a fat check in my purse from Finn. It's
going to go a long way with purchasing hay for
the mustangs."

Her remark pulled him away from his swirling thoughts and he glanced over to see she was

resting her head against the back of the seat. The light from the dashboard softly illuminated her face and he couldn't deny that with each hour and day he spent with her, she grew more lovely to him.

"When it comes to horses, Finn is a softy."

She turned slightly toward him. "Did you know he wants to breed a mustang bloodline into the ranch's remuda string?"

"Yes. But Dad and Grandfather will never allow it."

"But why? I can only see it making the herd more disease resistant. Stronger and more resilient."

Clancy shrugged. "They have their own mindset. Where the remuda is concerned they're pretty much old school and they feel the integrity and reputation of the ranch's horse division might be compromised by not holding on to the true quarter horse foundation."

"Well, Finn can't be happy about that."

"He isn't. But he understands he works for the family. Not for himself."

By now they'd reached Olivia's house and he parked the truck near the front-yard gate. After killing the engine, he turned to her.

"Would you rather I go back home tonight?"

Her brows lifted with faint surprise. "No. Is that what you want to do?"

"No. But I—" Pausing, he shrugged. "This evening, before we left to go to the Horn, I got the impression that you think sex is all I want from you."

She studied him for a moment before she leaned across the console and slipped her arms around his neck. "Have you ever considered that sex might be all I want from you?"

Clancy was stunned at how much that idea bothered him. Even though he wanted to keep their relationship safely away from anything serious, it hurt to think that all she might want him for was sexual pleasure. He wanted to mean more than that to her. Because she definitely meant more than that to him. He didn't exactly know what his feelings were yet. But something was inside him, pushing him closer and closer to her.

"Is it?" he asked huskily.

"No," she admitted. "I like your company."

His heart made a strange little wince. "I like your company, too."

She kissed him softly before easing out of his embrace. "Let's go in," she invited huskily.

After leaving the truck, they hurried across the cold yard and into the house. In the living room, a small fire was still burning low behind the safety screen pulled across the fireplace, casting a golden-orange glow over the furniture.

Before Olivia could say a word he removed both their coats, then wrapped his arms around her and walked her backward until her calves were pressed against the couch.

With the warmth of the fire spreading over

them, he lowered her onto the long length of cushions, then stretched out beside her.

With a heady sigh, she pulled him close and as Clancy found her mouth with his, he realized that the only place he felt truly at home was in her arms.

Did that mean he loved her? That his heart was finally beginning to trust her again?

When she'd walked out of his life, she'd taken ten years of hopes and dreams from him. Surely he deserved the time to decide whether he wanted to make a lifelong promise to her.

Chapter Nine

Clancy ended up spending the night with Olivia and the next morning, as the two of them were finishing breakfast, the dogs began barking loudly out in the front yard.

Looking around, Clancy said, "I think I hear a vehicle. Are you expecting company?"

"No. Unless—" Her eyes suddenly widened with excitement and she jumped to her feet. "It must be Ezra! He might have a horse for me!"

Snatching, a work coat from a peg by the door,

she hurried out of the house, leaving Clancy to follow at a slower pace.

By the time he walked to the front of the house, a truck and trailer had parked in the driveway. At the side of the driver's door, Olivia was giving a tall man in a gray cowboy hat a tight bear hug.

When she finally realized he was standing behind them, she turned and quickly introduced the two men.

"Ezra, this is my—uh—boyfriend, Clancy. And Clancy, this is my dear neighbor, Ezra."

Clancy politely stepped up to shake the older man's hand and was immediately struck by how strong and young the man appeared to be. Olivia had told him that her neighbor was in his early seventies, but to Clancy, he looked more like a man in his fifties.

"Nice to meet you, Ezra. I see you've brought Olivia a horse."

He grinned. "The last lot number to go and

by then most of the buyers had left to go home. Got him for a steal."

"Is he gentle and broke to ride?" Clancy felt compelled to ask. After all, Olivia's safety was his first and foremost concern.

Ezra looked thoroughly insulted. "You think I'd buy her anything that wasn't?"

Olivia gave the old man's arm a placating squeeze. "Of course you wouldn't, Ezra. Clancy wasn't doubting your judgment. He just can't help being a ranch manager."

"Sorry, Ezra. I really wasn't doubting your judgment. But I guess my question made it sound that way."

Seemingly appeased by Clancy's apology, Ezra reached out and gave Clancy's shoulder a pat. "Forget it. I'm just an old testy man who spouts off before he thinks. Come on and help me unload him."

After they'd turned the big chestnut safely into a stall in the barn, Olivia went to the house to collect her checkbook. While they waited for her to return, the two men stood watching the horse.

Resting his boot on the bottom rung of the fence, Clancy looked over at the older man. "I'd pay you for the horse myself. But I don't think she'd be too happy with me if I did."

"Heck, I'd like to just give her the horse. And I considered the idea of refusing to take her check," Ezra replied. "But she wouldn't be happy with me, either. Olivia is full of pride. And she's an independent little thing. But you've known her for a long time. I'm not telling you anything."

He was learning that and a whole lot more about Olivia, Clancy thought. And the more he learned about her, the more he learned about himself. Earlier, when the blaze-face gelding had emerged from the trailer and sniffed her hand, he'd never seen Olivia look so happy and excited. He'd wished more than anything that he could bring her that same sort of happiness.

But how could he? She didn't want anything his money could buy.

"She's different from the young woman I knew back in our college days," Clancy said thoughtfully.

"Hmm. She probably wouldn't appreciate me talking about her personal life. But since it's you, I figure it would be okay." Pulling a pack of gum from his shirt pocket, Ezra took his time peeling a piece and popping it into his mouth. "She hasn't made out too well with the men in her life. First her dad, then her brother, and then a no-account husband. And, well, she figures she's the only person she can truly trust."

Ezra's comment left a dead, heavy feeling in the middle of Clancy's chest. "She trusts you, Ezra."

The older man batted a hand through the air. "A little. But not completely. Not me or you."

Once again Ezra's words cut into Clancy. All this time he'd been telling himself he couldn't quite give all his trust to Olivia. He'd never stopped to consider that she might be having the same reservations about him. Clearly the men in her life had let her down. Was she thinking that he'd let her down, too?

Clancy was wondering how he could reply to Ezra's remarks, or even if he should, when Olivia suddenly walked into the barn.

Smiling broadly, she handed Ezra the check. "I put a little extra on it for your fuel cost. Thanks for taking the trouble to do all this for me."

"You didn't have to give me this today." As Ezra slipped the check into his shirt pocket, he exchanged a pointed glance with Clancy. "You could've waited if need be."

She gave the older man's arm an affectionate squeeze. "I've never been so happy to write a check. You've made my day, Ezra. Uh—by the way, does the horse have a name?"

"It's on his registry papers. I'll go get them out of the truck before I forget to give them to you."

Ezra left the barn and as Olivia moved closer to the stall to peer at the horse, Clancy stood next to her side.

"Isn't he gorgeous? I can't wait to ride him. But first I've got to buy a saddle and tack. And eventually I'll have to get a trailer to haul him in. I suppose the first thing I need to do today is drive into town and purchase feed and hay." Her excited string of words came to an end and she cast a questioning glance up at him. "Maybe you could help me with that?"

Feeling encouraged, he slipped his arm across the back of her waist. "I'd be happy to help you with all of it. Whatever you want, I'll get it."

She scowled at him. "That's not what I meant. I don't want you to buy anything for me. All I want is advice about his feed. What kind, how much, that sort of thing."

Her attitude should've filled him with relief. Being wealthy, he and his brothers had always had to wonder if they were loved for their money or themselves. Clearly, Olivia wasn't impressed with his bank account and that was probably a good thing. But on the other hand, he wished he had the right to buy for her, to give her all the things she needed and wanted.

You want to treat her as your wife, Clancy. Yet you don't have the guts to marry her. You can't keep straddling the fence. Sooner or later you're going to have to jump to one side or the other.

Trying to ignore the voice going off in his head, he said, "Okay, I can help you with that, Olivia. But why won't you let me help you with the other things? The cost associated with having a horse is expensive."

Her gaze left his face to settle on the horse. "I won't be your kept woman, Clancy. Not ever. I have more respect for myself than that."

Stung by her words, his hand tightened on the side of her waist. "But I—"

His words stopped as Ezra suddenly reappeared in the barn with the horse's registration papers and Clancy knew the chance to say more to her was over for now.

Later that afternoon, Clancy drove Olivia to town so that she could purchase the items she needed to feed her new horse. While there, they grabbed a burger at the Grubstake and by the time they finished the meal and drove back to Olivia's place, the day was nearly over.

Clancy helped her stack the feed and hay in a room in the barn, then rationed a portion to the horse. Once they were finished with the chores, Olivia expected Clancy to announce it was time for him to head back to the Silver Horn. Instead, he returned to the house with her and suggested they have a cup of coffee before he made the drive home.

She was standing at the cabinet, spooning coffee grounds into a filter, when he walked up behind her. "You don't really have to make the coffee. Unless you'd like a cup. I just used the excuse to talk to you."

Frowning slightly, she darted a glance over her shoulder. "We've been together all afternoon. You've had all sorts of opportunities to talk to me."

"I know. But I wanted us to be alone—without any distractions."

It made little difference that she'd spent the whole night before wrapped in his arms, the fact that his hard, male body was brushing against hers was enough to make her heart thump into a faster rhythm.

Resting her palms against the middle of his broad chest, she tilted her head back and smiled at him. "Okay. What did you want to talk to me about?"

"You. And what you said this morning out in the barn—about being a kept woman." His hands came up to rest on the tops of her shoulders. "That cut deep, Livvy. I don't offer to buy you things just because I think I owe it to you or that I own you."

Breathing deeply, she scanned his face. "I'm sorry if I insulted you, Clancy. That wasn't my intention."

He shook his head. "I wasn't exactly insulted. But your words were— It made me feel like you took your hand and shoved me aside."

A wad of tangled emotions was suddenly choking her. "I know you don't understand me, Clancy. And I'm sorry if I say things in the wrong way. But I've learned what's best for me. It's important for me to be self-sufficient."

"In other words, you don't want a man taking care of you. No matter his reason."

Uncertain where his comment was leading, her heart pounded even harder. "Is that what you want, Clancy? To take care of me?"

He grimaced. "Well, would that be so wrong? It's no secret that I have more than enough money to help you with horses, cattle, your house or vehicle—whatever you might need. It would make me happy to give to you. It would make me happy if you'd accept it."

A part of her was deeply touched by everything he was saying, while the other part wanted to pound her fist against his shoulder.

To keep from doing the latter, she turned back to the cabinet and pushed the on switch to the coffeemaker. "That's what a husband does for his wife, Clancy. And you're not my husband."

Long moments passed in silence, and then she felt the front of his body press into the back of hers. The solid heat was both comforting and disturbing, and she was torn between wanting to fling herself into his arms or run to the other side of the room.

"Is that what you want, Olivia? For us to be married?"

His voice was husky and threaded with an anguish that spoke volumes to Olivia.

"I don't let myself think about marriage very

much," she told him. "There's no point in it. Not when I already know how you feel about me."

"What do you mean? How do I feel?"

"You don't want to marry me. You've never forgiven me for breaking our engagement. And even if you could, you'd still be afraid I might do something like that to you again."

"Can you blame me?"

His hands began to knead her shoulders and it suddenly dawned on her that he truly wanted her to be open with him. Even if she had to tell him something he'd rather not hear.

She sighed. "That was a long time ago. I've changed. Since then I've learned about life and myself. If I had to do it all over, I'd probably handle everything differently. And I expect you might, too."

"Maybe," he replied. "I'm certain of one thing, though. I should've put up a bigger fight, instead of letting you just walk away."

Turning, she dared to look into his eyes. The

green depths were full of shadowy doubts and she wondered if he would ever be able to look at her with love and certainty. If he was still holding on to the past after ten years, how did she expect him to let go of it now?

"I want to be with you, Clancy, but sometimes I ask myself if I'm walking down a losing street."

Groaning, he pulled her into his arms and cradled her head against his chest. "Oh Livvy, I don't want you to feel that way. Neither one of us is losing anything, are we? We don't have to be married for things to be good for us."

His words tore at her heart and reminded her of all the times down through the years that a man had disappointed her, had left her wounded and lost. And those memories were enough to fight the tears burning her throat.

"Clancy, you assume that I want us to get married. But you're wrong. I'd never marry a man who doesn't trust me. So I guess we're stuck like this until one of us can't stand it any longer."

"You make it sound so hopeless."

She eased her head back to look at him and as her gaze took in his dear, familiar features, her heart felt like a cold stone, sinking lower and lower.

"I didn't say that. You did."

His hand stroked the back of her hair and Olivia closed her eyes as a mixture of sensations overwhelmed her.

"I don't want it to be like that between us, Livvy. I want to put the past in the past. But I have to look at things as they really are. Your job could move you away at any time. And I understand how much your position with the BLM means to you."

She opened her eyes and looked at him. "I worked hard and sacrificed more than you can imagine to get to where I am now. My job is everything to me—just like yours is to you. I won't give it up. If that's what you're asking."

"I'm not asking," he said flatly, then dropping his hold on her, he walked over to the table and reached for his hat where he'd left it and his coat on the seat of a chair. "I think I'd better go. Before we say too much."

He paused to lever the gray hat onto his head and she walked toward him. "You're leaving angry?" she asked.

A wry smile slanted his lips. "I'm not angry, Olivia. Are you?"

No, she was terribly sad. "I'm not angry. I'm wishing the day wasn't over. I'm wishing you could stay the night with me again and we could forget all of this for a while."

Stepping closer, he bent his head and pressed a brief kiss on her lips. "I wish I could stay, too. But a cattle buyer will be at the ranch early in the morning. Dad expects me to deal with him."

"Oh. Well, maybe next time."

He placed another kiss on her forehead before he turned and shouldered on his coat. "I'll call you soon."

A call now and then, a night here and there. As long as she remained in a relationship with Clancy, it would be the most she could hope for. Was that all that she wanted for herself? But what else was there? She certainly hadn't felt like dating since her divorce, and she doubted that was going to change once Clancy left her. She should probably just grab every chance she could to be with him.

Her coat was hanging on the back of a nearby chair. As she pulled it on, she tried not to sound as bleak as she felt. "I'll walk you to the truck."

Outside the sun was quickly disappearing and the wind had grown even colder. By the time he kissed her one last time and climbed into the truck, she was shivering. But even after he drove away, she didn't go directly into the house.

Instead, she walked out to the barn, the dogs trailing at her heels.

Inside the old wooden structure, she peered into the stall at the big red horse. His registered name was TR Flaming Dash and she'd decided to simply call him TR. "Come here, boy," she crooned to him. "I have another treat down in my pocket."

The horse left the pile of hay he'd been munching on and walked over to her. Olivia stepped up on the bottom rung of the fence and before she could tear the peppermint candy from its plastic wrapper, the animal was nosing her hand, begging for the sweet treat.

"We're going to be the best of buddies, TR."

As though he understand he'd found a home to stay, the horse stuck his nose beneath her arm and rubbed his cheek against the front of her coat. Olivia gently stroked his face and as she did, a tear slipped from her eye.

She might not ever truly belong in Clancy's

home or his life, but she had her own home and a good job. She had animals that loved and needed her. And mostly, she had her self-respect. She didn't need a husband to make her feel blessed. But that didn't mean she'd given up on wanting one.

A week later, on Thursday afternoon, Olivia was in the break room at work, resting her head on the tabletop when a hand came to rest on her shoulder.

"Are you okay, Olivia?"

Raising up, Olivia tried to blink away the drowsiness that had suddenly overcome her minutes before. "Oh, Bea, thank goodness you came in here. I was on the verge of falling asleep. The last thing I need is for the boss to walk through here and catch me napping."

The young woman waved away Olivia's words. "The boss is rarely ever in town. Besides, you give the department far more hours than necessary."

Wiping a hand over her face, Olivia pushed herself to her feet and picked up a half-eaten sandwich from the tabletop. "Well, I have a stack of paperwork to tend to. I need to get to it."

"You look pale and tired," Beatrice remarked as she studied Olivia closely. "Are you sure you're not sick?"

Actually, this past week Olivia hadn't exactly been feeling like herself. She'd never felt so tired in her life and by the time the afternoon arrived it was a chore to keep her eyes open. "I'm not sick. A long rest on the couch is what I need."

The secretary watched Olivia toss the sandwich into the trash bin. "Looks like you're not eating, either. Olivia, do you think you might be pregnant?"

Stunned by Beatrice's suggestion, Olivia stared at the younger woman. "Pregnant! Why, no! I mean—it's impossible."

Beatrice shrugged, then glanced at the door as though she wanted to make sure no one could overhear them. "Well, I didn't mean to speak out of turn. I'm just concerned about you, that's all. This past week you've not seemed yourself and I know that you've been seeing Clancy quite a bit. But if the two of you aren't that close then it must be something else making you sluggish."

As Olivia considered Beatrice's suggestion, a warm flush spread up her neck and onto her face. *Close* couldn't begin to describe her relationship with Clancy. Each time they were together, they wound up in bed. But she was on the Pill. She couldn't be pregnant!

The idea turned her legs to rubber and she sank back into the chair and drew in several long breaths.

"I don't think— Oh, surely it must be something else," she muttered as much to herself as she did to Beatrice.

Beatrice shook her head. "I'm thinking you should see a doctor, Olivia. You might need some extra iron or something."

Extra iron? If she was pregnant with Clancy's child she was going to need a heck of a lot more than an iron tablet, Olivia thought with dismay.

"You're right." Forcing herself to her feet, she patted Beatrice on the shoulder before heading out of the break room. "Thanks for your concern, Bea. I promise I'll make an appointment."

By the time Olivia left the field office that evening, she was so consumed with the thought of seeing a doctor that she didn't wait to make an appointment with her gynecologist. Instead, she went straight to a twenty-four-hour clinic and waited for the first available physician to give her a checkup.

An hour and a half later, she left the building in a daze. Beatrice had guessed correctly. Olivia's fatigue and lack of appetite was a result of her being pregnant. She was going to have a baby! Clancy's baby!

She'd not seen him since he'd left her house several nights ago when they'd had the discussion about money and trust and marriage. Since then, she'd tried not to think about his lack of commitment to their relationship. She wanted to believe that eventually, he'd come to realize how much she cared for him and that she was a different woman than the one who'd left him all those years ago. She continued to hope he'd come to understand that he could trust her with his heart.

But how could she expect him to make a permanent commitment to her when she'd never really made one to him? Instead of convincing him that she was willing to trust her heart to him a second time, she'd made a point of how much her independence and job meant to her. And now—well, the baby was going to change everything. For her and for him.

By the time she arrived home and finished her outside chores, she decided that it would hardly help matters to wait about contacting Clancy. Before she could change her mind, she picked up the phone and punched his number.

It rang so many times she was expecting the call to go to his voice mail, when he suddenly answered.

"Did I catch you at a bad time?" she asked.

"No. I was just leaving Dad's study. I wanted to get out here on the staircase landing before I answered. Is anything wrong?"

Drawing in a long breath, she closed her eyes. "No. Not exactly. I wanted to see if you could meet me somewhere tomorrow for lunch. Or whenever you can make it to town. I need to talk to you about something."

There was a long stretch of silence before he finally said, "My afternoon is tied up tomorrow. I might make it to the Grubstake in the morning about nine. But if it's something really important, maybe we should wait until tomorrow night. I'll come to your place."

That long of a wait would be agonizing, but telling him about the baby in a quiet, private place would be much better than a crowded diner.

"All right," she said. "I'll see you tomorrow night, then."

There was another long pause and then he said in an impatient voice, "Olivia, what is this about? Can't you tell me over the phone?"

She rubbed at the frown creasing the middle of her forehead. "I can't. If it's too much trouble for you to come over—"

"I didn't say that. You've just taken me by surprise, that's all. If this is about that discussion we had the other night—"

"It isn't. Not really."

She could hear him heave out a heavy breath. No doubt his mind was spinning with questions, she thought. But she figured that once he learned about the baby, it was going to be doing much more than spinning. He was probably going to be livid. He might even accuse her of getting pregnant on purpose. But she'd deal with all of that later, she promised herself.

"This past week has been hectic, Livvy. I'm sorry if you think I've been ignoring you. I've been trying to find a break to see you."

Her hand shook as she held the phone to her ear. "It's not that, Clancy. We'll talk tomorrow night. Right now, I've got to get off the phone. Cleo is howling for her supper."

She gave him a quick goodbye, then ended the phone connection. Next to her, the calico cat sat quietly, watching her with accusing eyes.

"Okay, Cleo, so I told a little fib. You're not howling. I'm sorry I used you for an excuse. But what does it matter, anyway? You don't even like Clancy."

The calico stuck her nose in the air, then promptly jumped off the couch. Olivia watched the cat leave the room, then dropped her head in her hands.

There was no use in wondering or trying to pretend. She was in love with Clancy. She'd never stopped loving him. But that fact hardly helped matters. As far as she could see, it only made things worse. Because Clancy didn't return her love. And now she was going to have his baby. A baby he'd never planned on having. With a woman he didn't trust. Dear God, could it get any worse?

Chapter Ten

Clancy didn't know why, today of all days, his grandfather, Bart, had insisted they drive up to the land he'd purchased on the Rock Mountain range. A stack of sale negotiations was lying on Clancy's desk, waiting for him to go over before he sent them to Jett's office. Finn was expecting him to contact a dealer for a new horse walker and his dad was hounding him to make a trip to Ely to purchase another two hundred head of cows to put on Antelope Range. And then there was Olivia's request to see him tonight.

Frankly, he was still knocked a little sideways by her call. Not that it was surprising to hear from her. Since they'd become involved again, she called him occasionally and he made it a point to keep in touch with her throughout the week. But something about her voice had sounded strained, even a little urgent.

"Clancy, wasn't that the turnoff back there?"

Clancy turned a blank look over at his grandfather. "What?"

"Damn it, where is your head today? I said I think you missed the turnoff. But that was a half mile back by now."

Cursing under his breath, Clancy glanced in the truck's rearview mirror, then jammed on the brakes and made a U-turn in the middle of the empty highway.

"Why didn't you say something before now?"

Bart shook his head. "I did. You weren't listening."

No, he'd been too busy thinking about Olivia

and what this meeting of hers was all about. Had she decided she didn't want to remain in a relationship with him? The mere idea left him cold and lost.

You more or less told her you didn't want to get married. What do you expect her to do, Clancy? Waste her young years waiting on you. There're plenty of men out there who'd be more than happy to marry Olivia and give her a home and family. Maybe you need to think about that.

"Sorry, Grandfather. I have a lot on my mind. Dad's having a fit for me to go to Ely and take a look at those cows he's wanting. And—"

"You don't have to go on, Clancy. I'm not deaf or blind. The whole family is always pulling and pushing at you. That's why you're the only one of the boys who could ever deal with being the Silver Horn's manager. Your brothers would break under the stress."

Bart had never been one to give praise. In fact, he was usually complaining and giving orders to everyone in the family. To hear this sort of compliment from the old man this morning, somewhat made up for dragging Clancy on this unnecessary trip.

"I'm used to it."

"Yeah, I guess you are," Bart said as Clancy pulled into the entrance of the property. "We started training you for the job before you ever knew you wanted it. Now that you've worked at it for a few years, do you ever want to quit and do something else?"

Bart's question caught Clancy by complete surprise. "You mean leave the ranch?"

"That's what I meant."

Clancy frowned. "No. That notion never crosses my mind. Why would I? I love this land as much as you. I want the ranch to continue to flourish—for all of us."

The older man didn't make any sort of reply and Clancy glanced over to see he was nodding silently.

"You've never disappointed me, Clancy. I hope you never do."

Even though Olivia made passionate love to him whenever they were together, he was always aware that she was holding a part of herself back. At times, he'd even caught her looking at him with eyes that were clouded with disappointment. Clancy didn't understand how he'd let her down or even when, but he desperately wished he could hear the same words from her that his grandfather had just spoken to him.

Once they'd driven as far as the rough road could take them, Bart insisted on hiking up the last of the rise until they reached the mountain meadow where Clancy and Olivia had explored so many weeks ago.

"Where's the mine located from here?" Bart asked as the two men gazed around at the stand of pines growing densely at the edge of the opening.

"Follow me and I'll show you."

Clancy guided him to the south side of the rim and pointed downward through the trees. "See the water glistening through the trees? That's the little lake we found. The mine is probably fifty or sixty feet over to the right of it."

"Let's go have a look," Bart said.

Clancy stared at him in disbelief. "Grandfather, are you serious? It's rough going getting down there. And you—"

"I'm just as spry as I was before the stroke. Lilly has seen to that. I can make it."

Rafe's wife had been Bart's therapy nurse after he'd suffered the stroke that had affected the mobility on one side of his body. For some reason, the two of them had bonded almost instantly and she'd managed, where many had failed, to encourage the old man to work hard and get himself back into physical shape.

"If you end up breaking a bone, I'll be to blame," Clancy argued. "And how the hell would I ever get you out of this place?"

"How would I get *you* out?" Bart retorted.

Seeing he'd never be able to talk his grandfather out of climbing down the mountainside, he shook his head. "All right. We'll go. But we're going to keep this little trek to ourselves. If Dad ever found out I went along with you on this, he'd skin my hide. And yours, too, probably."

Bart chuckled and patted Clancy on the shoulder. "Don't worry, son, no one will ever know but you and me."

For the next few minutes as they descended the wooded slope, it became evident to Clancy that he'd greatly misjudged his grandfather's strength and dexterity. Bart had no trouble staying right behind him. And when they finally reached the entrance of the old mine shaft, he wasn't breathing any harder than Clancy.

"I've seen some old mines in my time," he said, looking from the hole in the side of the mountain to the dammed water. "But I've never seen a setup quite like this one."

Clancy pointed to a spot several yards on down the mountain. "That's where Olivia and I found several pieces of the flume."

"Too bad we couldn't have seen this old mine back in the day. When the ore was being washed." He walked over to the opening of the mine shaft and peered into the dark hole. "Olivia was right about this place."

Surprised that his grandfather even mentioned Olivia's name, Clancy stepped over to his side. "What do you mean?"

Bart glanced over at him. "She said someone here once had a dream. That woman of yours is perceptive. I like that about her."

"It's nice that you've decided you like Olivia," Clancy told him, then shrugged. "But as for the dream...the way I see it someone was looking for a fortune in gold or silver. That's not a dreamer, that's a fortune hunter."

Turning away from the dark hole, Bart frowned at him. "Could be. But on the other hand, the miner might have wanted to find silver or gold for reasons other than just being rich. Could be he wanted a wife and family. Or maybe he already had one and he was trying to provide and give them a better life."

Bart's comment caused Clancy to pause and ponder. He'd never considered that his grandfather thought in such romantic terms. From the time he'd been old enough to think about such things, he'd seen his grandfather as a man driven to possess and acquire more wealth. Just for the sake of having it.

"Is that why you've worked so hard to expand the Silver Horn? For your family?"

A wry smile crossed Bart's face. "I never needed wealth for myself, Clancy. I'm surprised you haven't already figured that out about your old grandfather. It's family that gives a man purpose, Clancy. But I shouldn't have to explain that to you. You should already know that, too."

Feeling like a fraud, Clancy moved away from

his grandfather and stood staring at the pine forest where he and Olivia had searched for scattered remnants of the flume. That day they'd explored this land together, he'd felt very connected to her and since then she'd swiftly and steadily begun to consume his thoughts and feelings. She'd even started pushing herself into his hopes and dreams for the future. Yet each time he imagined making her his wife, cold resentment would wash through him and his heart would revolt at the idea. She'd vowed her love to him once, but that hadn't been enough to keep her from walking away. He had little assurance that she wouldn't do it a second time.

Clancy heard his grandfather's footsteps approaching him from behind and then Bart said, "Clancy, I've come to a decision about this piece of mountain land."

Curious now, Clancy, glanced over his shoulder at Bart. "What sort of decision? You want

Rafe to check the fencing and haul some cattle up here?"

"No. Nothing like that. I've decided I'm going to give this land to you and Olivia."

Momentarily staggered by his grandfather's announcement, Clancy stared at him in wonder. "Me and Olivia? I don't understand. Why?"

"Because I think you two would appreciate it more than anyone else. You can make your home up there on the meadow. And this old mine will be yours. You can choose to dig it out, close it up, or simply leave it and let your kids mine it one day. Doesn't matter to me."

Clancy couldn't believe what he was hearing. Bart had never given land to any of his children or grandchildren before. The fact that he'd chosen Clancy as the one to be generous with was more than he could comprehend.

"But, Grandfather, Olivia and I—we—I don't have plans to marry her. And I wouldn't feel right accepting this land with you assuming that

Olivia and I were going to stay together and have a family."

Instead of appearing upset by Clancy's confession, Bart smiled with clever confidence. "Right now you might be thinking you're not going to marry the woman. But you will. And the two of you will be happy up here."

Dear God, was Bart's thinking going haywire? He'd seemed to recover fully from his stroke and before today had never given any indications of mental confusion. But now the old man seemed to be thinking he could predict the future.

Frowning, Clancy looked away from him and muttered, "I don't know where you're getting that idea. But I—"

"I've lived more than eighty years. The night of Evan's birthday part I watched you two together and I understand about these things."

Clancy's throat suddenly felt as if he'd tried to swallow a baseball. "You understand that she broke our engagement all those years ago. That she hurt me like nothing or no one has ever hurt me. How the hell am I supposed to make her my wife and not worry that she'll leave me all over again?"

Bart cursed a streak under his breath. "Then what the hell are you doing with her? You figure that out, Clancy. And then you'll see your old grandfather is right."

Before Clancy could make a sensible retort to that, Bart pointed back up the mountainside. "I've seen enough. Let's climb out of here and head back to the ranch."

This time, as they headed up the slope of the mountain, it was his grandfather who took the lead. Evidently Bart wasn't afraid of falling. Or maybe he figured Clancy would be right behind to catch him if he slipped. One thing was clear, his grandfather believed Clancy would never disappoint him. And that was a heavy load to bear.

* * *

Olivia had wanted to get home from work early enough to shower and change before Clancy arrived, but finishing an urgent report had kept her at the office later than usual. After that she'd taken the time to stop at a nearby deli for a take-out meal of fried chicken.

She'd been home five minutes when she'd received a text from Clancy saying he was fewer than ten minutes away. Now she was scurrying to simply brush her hair, put on lipstick and place the food on the table before he arrived.

When his knock sounded at the back door, she rubbed her sweaty hands down the front of her jeans and told herself not to be nervous or afraid. She'd already survived many adversities and hurdles in her life. And as far as she was concerned, the baby wasn't either of those things. It was a blessing. Something to be celebrated.

"Come in, Clancy." She swung the door wide

enough for him to enter. "Thank you for coming on such short notice."

"Hello, beautiful." He stepped inside the warm
kitchen and as soon as she shut the door behind
him, he instantly pulled her into his arms and
placed a long, thorough kiss on her lips.

"Mmm. That was quite a greeting," she murmured when he finally lifted his head.

"I've been thinking about you all day," he said
in a low, suggestive voice. "And I've been wanting to do that all day."

She could've told him she'd been doing more
than thinking about him today, she'd literally
been obsessing over him. But she didn't want
to get into the reason for his visit just yet.

"I'm glad," she told him softly, "because I've
been needing that all day."

Taking him by the arm, she urged him into
the center of the kitchen where he spotted the
food she'd laid out on the table.

"It's late," he said. "I assumed you'd already eaten."

"I was late getting home," she explained, "and I thought we might eat together. Unless you've already had dinner at the Silver Horn."

Turning toward her, he gathered her hands in his. "I don't want to seem impatient, Livvy, but last night you said you needed to talk. I'd rather get that out of the way before we eat."

Get it out of the way, she thought dismally. Like a dreaded chore he wanted to finish quickly. Well, she supposed there was no way to delay the unavoidable now.

Glancing away from him, she breathed deeply and tried to brace her bumpy nerves.

"Okay. Let's go into the living room. There should be a few hot coals left in the fireplace. I'll throw a few logs on."

"I'll do it," he told her. "You sit."

They moved to the front of the house and Olivia made herself comfortable on the couch while Clancy shed his hat and coat, then built up the fire. As he piled on the logs and levered them with a poker, she watched the lean muscles of his shoulders bunch and stretch, and the sight stirred desire deep within her.

This man had once put an engagement ring on her finger. The same ring that was hidden away in her dresser drawer like a forgotten keepsake of happier times. When he'd slipped the diamond on her hand all those years ago, he'd promised her everything. Now all he wanted to give her was his body and a bit of his time. She supposed she had no one to blame but herself for her loveless situation. She'd had his heart once. Maybe it was hopeless to expect him to forget the past and give his love to her again.

"That should warm things up in here," he said.

Turning away from the flames, he walked over to join her on the couch. As he stretched his long legs out in front of him, she watched his face and tried to imagine his reaction when he learned he was going to be a father.

"Thank you, Clancy. It feels wonderful."

"Were you working outside today?"

"During the morning. This afternoon I was working on reports. If I had my choice, I'd rather be outside in the cold. But I have to report everything I see or my job would be meaningless."

He shifted slightly on the cushion so that he was facing her comfortably and for one second Olivia considered throwing herself in his arms and putting off the news about the baby until later. But that wouldn't be fair to him. Nor, in the long run, would it help her.

"So what did you need to talk to me about? Frankly, I've been a little worried since you called. You sounded a bit strained on the phone. Has something been going on at work? Has Wes or some other guy been coming on to you?"

Was he jealous? She doubted it. He didn't care

enough to be that possessive of her. "No. All the men I work with are very respectful to me. This has nothing to do with my job. It's—" Needing something to hang on to, she reached over and curled her fingers tightly around his. "I haven't been feeling too well this past week. And Bea convinced me to make a visit to the doctor."

A look of real concern came over his face. "Olivia! Why didn't you tell me you've been ill?"

"I only saw the doctor late yesterday afternoon. And—"

Before she could continue, he interrupted, "Is it something serious?"

Serious? It was definitely that, Olivia thought, but not in the way he was thinking. Lifting her gaze to his, she tried to give him a reassuring smile, but she could feel her lips trembling. "No. Actually, the doctor says I'm healthy and…pregnant."

It took a moment for the last word to sink in

and when it did, he scooted to the edge of the cushion and stared at her in disbelief. "Pregnant! But how? You take the Pill. You can't be pregnant!"

"I told the doctor the exact same thing. He explained that there are certain circumstances that can cause the Pill to fail. Even eating certain foods, missing a pill or taking it at a different time of the day, antibiotic use—or sometimes a woman ovulates in spite of the Pill. I'm thinking my case must be the latter. Which tells me that this baby was simply meant to be."

He continued to stare at her and then his head swung back and forth. "I never expected this to happen."

There was a rueful note in his voice and the sound pierced Olivia like a sharp icicle. Even though the practical part of her had known Clancy was going to be unhappy with this unexpected development, the woman in her, the deepest part of her heart had yearned for him to be pleased.

"Neither did I. I understand you trusted me to have reliable birth control." She cleared her throat in an attempt to rid her voice of its huskiness. "I'm sorry."

"It's not your fault. It's mine. I should have worn protection. But that hardly matters now."

Dropping his hold on her hands, he rose to his feet and suddenly Olivia felt as though a huge chasm was standing between them instead of a mere few inches.

"So how do you feel about this baby?" he asked. "Do you want to keep it?"

Amazed that he could even ask such a question, she shot to her feet. "What kind of question is that? It's my child! Of course I want to keep it!"

Unaffected by her sudden outburst, he simply looked at her. "How could I know? You just told me the other night that your job meant everything to you. A baby might interfere."

Stepping around him, she stalked over to the fireplace and stuck her fingers toward the heat radiating out from the flames in hopes it would melt the icy feeling that was quickly sweeping over her.

"Millions of women with babies work," she reasoned. "Will it interfere with your job?"

From somewhere behind her, he said, "That's hardly the question here. Or the point I was trying to make. You do a lot of strenuous work, walking and climbing. Pregnancy will no doubt put a damper on that."

As far as Olivia could see, he was the one trying to put a damper on her future. "I'm in great physical shape. Barring any complications, I'll manage just fine."

He didn't make any sort of reply to that. In fact, he remained quiet for so long that Olivia finally turned away from the fire to see he was standing in front of the picture window, staring out at the night sky.

"Clancy, you don't have to pretend with me. I never expected you to be happy about this. I'd hoped you might be a little pleased. But considering how you feel about me I realized that wouldn't be likely."

Frowning, he glanced over his shoulder at her before he turned and closed the distance between them. "How I feel about you? You couldn't possibly know how I feel. I don't know myself."

His blunt words were like a slap to her face. "Whether you know it or not, Clancy, your feelings are very clear to me. If you cared at all, if you felt one glimmer of love for me, you would've already taken me in your arms and told me that the baby is important to you. That I'm important to you. Instead, you're looking at me like a problem that you don't know how to fix."

Groaning, he shook his head. "Olivia, this is

a serious step in our lives. Do you expect me to be shouting 'yippee yi yay' and turning cartwheels?"

Pain and anger caused her teeth to snap together and her hands to clench. "I don't expect anything from you, Clancy. Nothing at all. So if that's what's worrying you—"

Before she could finish, he stepped forward and curved his hands around her upper arms. "Well, I expect something from you, Livvy. We're going to be married. And we're going to raise this child together."

Her mouth fell open, and then outrage had her jerking away from him and hurrying to the other side of the room. "Not on your life, Clancy Calhoun! We might raise this child together, but we sure as hell won't be doing it as a married couple."

His steely gaze bored into her. "You're saying you don't want to marry me?"

The incredulous tone in his voice angered her

even more. Did he think she was that desperate to have him as a husband? Or that he was such a catch that he couldn't believe any woman would actually turn him down? More than anything she wanted the baby to have two parents together in a real home filled with love. But no matter what Clancy was thinking at this moment, Olivia refused to let him use their child as a bargaining pawn to force her into marrying him.

"I can't say it any plainer."

He stalked over to her and she could see his jaw was rigid.

"You just told me you wanted this baby," he said flatly. "Why would you not want it to have a father?"

"You will be its father. You are its father. A marriage license can't change that."

He studied her for long moments and when she gazed back at him, she was relieved to see some of the anger draining out of him. She didn't want this to be a sparring match with the baby between them.

"I don't understand you, Livvy. You agreed to marry me once. Now that you're carrying my child, I'd think the baby would be enough to make you want to be my wife."

He couldn't know the pain his words were inflicting upon her heart. A person had to really love before they could hurt and Clancy wasn't hurting. He was angry and concerned and wanting his way, but his feelings weren't lying crushed on the floor like hers.

Turning her back to him, she said in a low, hoarse voice, "I made the mistake of marrying a man who didn't love me once. I won't do it a second time. I think I deserve more than that. My baby deserves more than that."

She could feel him inching toward her until the front of his body was nearly pressing into her back. And though a part of her wanted to turn and fling herself into his arms and promise him anything, she stared determinedly forward. The past ten years had taught her that she was the only person she could depend on. Not Clancy. Not any man.

"You don't want to remember that I loved you once very much. And what did I get in return from you? You broke our engagement—"

"Because of my mother. You know that!" she interrupted. "But you can't forgive me for it, can you? Your big Calhoun ego can't bear to think I chose my ailing mother over you."

Anger flashed in his eyes, then just as quickly it was gone and his head swung back and forth with disbelief. "Your mother died, Livvy. But you didn't come to me then or even try to contact me. Instead, you married someone else."

She bit down hard on her lip to keep from breaking into sobs. "Because I had sense enough to know that I could never be what you wanted me to be. Maybe I understood that all along—

even before Mother became ill. And maybe I understand it even better now."

"You're talking in riddles, Livvy. I don't understand what you mean. I don't even think you do."

Turning away from him she walked back over to the fireplace, even though it was useless to expect the heat to ease the cold emptiness in her heart.

"When you do finally marry, Clancy, you'll want your wife to be someone you can be proud of. You'll want her to be from a nice family and if she has a job, you'll want it to be a proper feminine job. Not one where your wife gets her hands in the soil or wades a creek and wonders how she can get water flowing for the people over in the next county."

He joined her on the fireplace hearth, but he didn't look at her, much less touch her. "You're getting way away from the issue, Olivia. A baby is coming. Our baby. Are you selfishly going to put your feelings before our child's?"

She looked over at him with a cutting glare and fought like crazy to keep from screaming at him. "Don't you try to lay the selfish thing on me, Clancy. You have no idea the sacrifices I've made in my life. Or the ones I will continue to make for my child. So why don't you go home to your fancy home and rich family and ask yourself where you were when I needed you the most!"

His expression clueless, he asked, "What? I—"

Her throat ached with unshed tears. "Please, leave now Clancy. I can't keep going over this. Not tonight."

He stared at her for several long seconds before he turned and gathered his coat and hat from where he'd left it on the chair.

As he skewered the gray hat down on his head, he started toward the door, while flinging a parting shot over his shoulder. "This isn't over, Olivia. It's just beginning."

Threats instead of promises to love and cherish, she thought sadly. She supposed she deserved that kick in the face for making the mistake of letting him back into her life a second time.

"Goodbye, Clancy."

He slammed out the door and she walked numbly back to the kitchen and began to put away the food she'd purchased for their supper. Maybe tomorrow she'd feel like eating. Maybe tomorrow her heart would quit aching and she could start planning a future without Clancy.

The thought brought her up short and she leaned against the cabinet counter and covered her face with both hands. She couldn't put Clancy out of her life. Not completely. They were going to have a baby together. That connection alone would force her to stay in contact with him. Even spend time with him.

Dear heaven, how could she watch him hold their baby while everything inside her would be aching to touch him, love him? It would be sheer agony. So why hadn't she accepted his proposal and made her dream of being his wife come true? she asked herself.

Because it hadn't been a proposal. It had been a decree, spoken without love. And even though she very much wanted her baby to have its father and mother living together as a family, she refused to marry a man who didn't love her.

Chapter Eleven

Nearly two weeks later, Clancy was sitting in his office staring blankly at the ledger sheet on the computer screen. In the past three months, the cost of alfalfa hay had skyrocketed and Rafe was already ordering more, and the winter was just getting started. Clancy was either going to have to pull funds from some other project to pay for extra hay or search for a cheaper seller. Which he doubted he could find this late in the year. Tomorrow would be the first day of

November. Any new hay crops would have to come all the way from southern California.

A light knock sounded on the door and Clancy looked up, surprised that anyone would be down at the office buildings at this time of night.

"Come in," he called.

Rafe hurriedly stepped in out of the cold and shut the door behind him. "Snowing again," he announced as he stomped his boots on a small rug. "The slopes over at Tahoe must be thrilled not to have to use the snow machines. This is turning out to be the wettest autumn we've had in years. And it couldn't come soon enough."

"It will certainly help the drought situation and the spring grass. I was just going over the hay situation. A hundred more ton is going to cost a heck of a lot, Rafe."

His younger brother walked over and took a seat in front of Clancy's desk. "I know. But we don't have much choice. The cows can't eat with snow on the ground. And we can't make money if they don't hold their weight."

Clancy wearily swiped a hand over his face. "That's true. I'll shuffle some funds around. We might have to forego drilling those two water wells for a while. Especially since we're getting by with the tanks we have right now."

Rafe pulled off his hat and hung it on his crossed knees. "Forget all that for the moment, I came down here to see why you missed dinner. Are you sick?"

Clancy frowned. "If I was sick I'd hardly be working."

Rafe cursed under his breath. "Well, there's hardly any need for you to be working at eight o'clock in the evening. In fact, you look like hell to me."

"Thanks," Clancy said drily. "At least, nothing about my looks has changed."

Rafe rolled his eyes toward the ceiling. "Don't you think this rift between you and Olivia has gone on long enough? She needs you now, Clancy, more than ever."

Clancy stared at him and wondered exactly how much his brother knew about the situation. "What do you mean by that?"

Rafe shrugged. "Dad told me that she's expecting a baby."

Grimacing, Clancy tossed the pen he'd been holding down on the desktop. "When I talked to him about Olivia I didn't realize he was going to start spreading the news."

"He's only shared it with me. And what difference does it make who he tells? Pretty soon Olivia will start showing and her condition will be evident to everyone."

"Yeah. You're right." He pushed out a weary sigh and leaned back in the desk chair. "But as for Olivia needing me, she doesn't. She's made that quite clear. She's also made it quite clear that she doesn't want to be my wife."

"Hmm. I wonder why."

Clancy shot his brother an annoyed look. "What does that remark mean?"

"It means that a woman wants to know she's loved for herself. She needs to know you want her to be your wife because you love her and want her in your life. Not just because she's carrying your child."

Shifting uncomfortably in his seat, Clancy stared over to one side of the room where a black leather couch and matching armchairs were grouped around a small fireplace. Once Clancy had returned from college and taken over the position as ranch manager, his grandfather had spared no expense in furnishing the office. Bart had always reasoned that it was important to give cattle and horse buyers the impression that everything on the Silver Horn was top-notch, especially the livestock.

Go home to your fancy home and rich family and ask yourself where you were when I needed you the most.

Olivia's parting words had been especially hard for him to take. Not just because he'd been angry with her. And not because she'd turned down his request for her to become his wife. He'd been stunned by the idea that he might have ever let her down. During those long years they'd been apart, Clancy had always thought of himself as the wronged party. She'd let him down. Not the other way around. So what had she meant? What could he have done differently?

You could have gone to her in Idaho, Clancy. You could have made sure that she and her mother had everything they needed. No matter how long it took, you could've showed her that you weren't going to let anything come between you and that you'd be there for her through thick and thin, through happiness and sorrows.

Clearing the gruffness from his voice, he said, "I realize you're more of an authority on wives and women than I am, Rafe. But you don't understand about Olivia. She's very independent and headstrong. She—"

Rafe interrupted with a burst of laughter. "And you think Lilly isn't? When we were dating she told me to get the hell out and not come back."

Clancy looked at his brother. "Well, clearly you did go back. And she married you."

"Only because I came to my senses. I realized I loved Lilly too much to lose her to another man. I don't think you want to see Olivia and your child with another man, either."

The thought of some other man loving and caring for Olivia and his baby was worse than trying to swallow barbed wire. Clancy couldn't bear it.

Did that mean he loved her? The deep down sort of love that his grandfather had felt when he'd married Clancy's grandmother? The kind of love his father had felt for his mother? And what if he did love Olivia in that same way? Clancy asked himself. Just because he loved her didn't mean he could trust her to always stay at his side.

"I don't want to think about that, Rafe. I don't want to think about Olivia and the baby anymore tonight. I've thought about them until I'm worn-out thinking. I—"

The rest of Clancy's remarks were suddenly interrupted as the phone on his desk rang.

"That's coming from the house," Clancy said to Rafe. "Lilly must be hunting you."

"Lilly would ring my cell. Better answer. It might be Grandfather."

Clancy especially didn't want to talk to his grandfather. In fact, these past few days since his split with Olivia, he'd deliberately been avoiding Bart. He wasn't up to having the old man chew a hole in him, much less facing the disappointment that would surely be in his eyes.

Reluctantly, he reached for the receiver. "Clancy here," he answered.

"Clancy, it's Finn. I just got off the phone with Evan. He's at Tahoe General. Something is wrong with Dad."

The serious tone in Finn's voice had Clancy freezing with fear. "With Dad! Why? What's wrong? Isn't Evan on duty tonight?"

"Yes. But Noreen contacted him. She and Dad had dinner together and they were heading back to her place when he started having chest pains. He's in Emergency now. Evan's waiting to hear word."

"Oh, God. Rafe is here with me now. The two of us will be right there, Finn."

He hung up the phone to see that Rafe had already risen to his feet and was staring anxiously at him.

"What's wrong?"

Leaping out of the chair, Clancy grabbed his hat and coat. "Dad. He's at Tahoe General. Let's go."

At the same time, more than thirty miles away at Olivia's house, she'd invited Ezra to supper and the two of them were finishing the last of the barbecued ribs she'd thrown into the slow-cooker early that morning before she'd left for work.

"I really shouldn't be eating like this," she told Ezra. "But this is the first day I've gotten through without a bout of nausea. Everything tastes good tonight."

Ezra grinned at her and Olivia realized her stand-in dad was as excited about her pregnancy as if it was going to be his own grandchild.

"I'm glad to hear it," he said. "I don't want you getting sick. You gotta stay healthy so that little one will grow strong."

She reached across the table and gave the back of his hand a reassuring pat. "I had a long visit with an obstetrician yesterday. He assures me that I'm fine and the baby is fine. So don't worry. In a few months I'll be asking you to change diapers and babysit."

The grin suddenly fell from his face. "I doubt

that. Once you marry Clancy, I'll probably never see you again."

She slanted him a pointed look. "That isn't likely. And even if by some miraculous chance I married Clancy, you will always be in my life."

He looked away from her, but not before she saw his eyes blink and Olivia knew he had to be thinking about his own son, who'd left the area years ago and rarely ever came back for visits. For some reason Ezra had never explained to Olivia why his son had broken ties with him.

"I'm glad to hear it, Livvy. Because I've sorta gotten used to you being around—feeding me like a king," he said.

Feeling far more emotional than she should be, Olivia rose to her feet and walked over to the cabinet counter. As she began making a pot of decaffeinated coffee, she said, "I haven't told you yet, but I got a big surprise at work today."

"A surprise? Was it a good one?"

Shrugging, Olivia didn't bother to turn to look at him. "A few months ago I would have called it wonderful. In fact, I would have been jumping with excitement. But now—everything is different."

"Maybe you'd better explain what this surprise was. 'Cause I'm not understanding you, Livvy."

With the coffee dripping, she turned to give him a wan smile. "I've been offered a big promotion. It's something I've had my eye on since I first went to work for the BLM. It would mean a lot more money. But mostly it would mean that my work would hold some real weight—even more than it does now."

A puzzled frown crossed Ezra's face. "And you're not happy about all that?"

"The job would require me to move to California. Far away from here."

He looked crestfallen. "Oh. And you don't want to do that?"

Smiling, she walked over to where he sat at

the table and gave his shoulders an affectionate hug. "And leave you? Never."

Much later that night at Tahoe General, Clancy and his brothers, along with their father's girl-friend, Noreen, were milling restlessly around the waiting area, trying not to think the worst. Three hours had passed since Orin had arrived in Emergency and the only word they'd received so far was that he was being treated and that a battery of tests were being done. Jett, Clancy's brother-in-law, had stayed for a while but Sassy was home with their son, J.J.

When a young doctor finally approached them, the brothers and Noreen circled around him, waiting anxiously for him to speak.

"Mr. Calhoun is stable and awake and has been transferred to a regular room. I expect to keep him here for the next two days. At least until I get to the bottom of what is causing all his discomfort."

"Does that mean he didn't have a heart attack?" Evan was the first to ask. "You would have put him in ICU if that was the case, right?"

The weary physician removed a pair of reading glasses and slipped them into the pocket on his lab coat. "Going by the first initial tests we've run, it doesn't appear to be a heart attack. But I'm not ready to rule that out completely until I run a few more tests. Right now we have the pain under control. And that's the way I want to keep things. When I learn the exact cause, then I can start treating it."

"Can we see him now, Doctor?" Finn asked.

"One of you can see him. But only for a brief visit. I don't want him exhausted with a bunch of talk. Now if you'll excuse me, I have another patient waiting."

They all thanked the doctor and after he'd walked away, Clancy and his brothers instinctively looked to Noreen. The attractive brunette immediately shook her head.

"As much as I'd like to see Orin, one of you should go. He's your father and he needs you now."

As soon as her words were out, Clancy could feel all eyes turn on him. "Why are you looking at me?" Clancy asked. "Rafe is Dad's pet. He'd rather see him."

"Not hardly!" Rafe exclaimed. "Evan was the first one here. He ought to go."

Finn stepped forward and latched a hand on Clancy's arm. "You're the oldest, Clancy. You've always been the leader. You're the one who should see Dad. We'll all wait here."

The leader. These past couple of weeks he'd hardly felt like a leader. He'd felt lost. Like a horse wandering around the range, like a horse wanting to go home, but not knowing which direction to take to find it.

His throat too tight to speak, Clancy nodded and hurried off to catch the elevator.

On the third floor, he found his father's room

at the end of a long wing. After a slight rap on the door, he stepped inside and stood staring at the bed where his father was resting on his side. Wires emerged from the neck of the hospital gown and eventually connected to a small machine standing next to the head of the bed.

As Clancy stepped forward he tried to keep his steps light against the tile floor, but Orin must have heard the sound of his boots anyway, because his eyes fluttered open to focus on his eldest son.

"Clancy. Come in."

His father's voice sounded a bit winded, as though an excessive amount of pressure was pushing the words out of him. A sheen of sweat covered his forehead, but at least there was color to his cheeks. For as far back as Clancy could remember, he couldn't recall ever seeing his father sick in bed. And certainly never hospitalized. Seeing him in such a vulnerable state shook Clancy to the very center of his being. Orin was the very anchor of the Calhoun family. He was too young and vital for his health to be threatened, Clancy thought.

Striding quickly to the bedside, he reached for his father's hand. "Dad. How are you feeling?"

"Better. At least I can get a decent breath now."

He squeezed his hand. "The boys are in the waiting room. And so is Noreen. She's very concerned about you. We all are."

"Doc says I'll be fine. Tell Noreen not to worry. Tell your brothers not to worry."

"The doctor would only allow one of us to see you." Clancy shook his head with dismay. "We offered the chance to Noreen, but everyone thought I should be the one to visit you."

"I'm glad," Orin replied. "I want to make sure you continue to take care of the ranch just as you always do."

A ball of emotion was suddenly choking Clancy, forcing him to try and swallow it away. And suddenly, as he watched his father's eyelids drift wearily downward, he understood what Olivia must have been feeling when she'd learned her mother had a serious disease. It must have shaken her entire world, just as it was shaking Clancy's world tonight to think his father might be dying.

Oh, God, Arlene Parsons had been dying, Clancy thought. And from what Olivia had told him she'd suffered through more than two years of treatment and pain before she'd finally succumbed to the disease. Olivia had endured all the worry and grief alone. She'd had no family to support her. And he'd been a jerk for letting his male pride get in the way. For not going to her and offering his help and his love. Sure she'd told him to move on and forget her, but now after all these years, he could see that she'd done it out of love. She'd not wanted to tie him down with the burdens of her family.

"You don't need to worry about the ranch, Dad. I'll see that everything keeps running smoothly.

And if necessary, I'll keep Grandfather in line. All you need to do is rest and get well. Is there anything I can get for you?"

A weak smile crossed his face. "How about three hundred head of mama cows?"

With a wry shake of his head, Clancy said, "It's good to see you still have your sense of humor."

His father's fingers tightened around his. "Don't worry, son, I'm going to be around to see your baby born—my grandchild. You just make Olivia see that she needs to be a part of our family. That's the best medicine you could give me."

Clancy couldn't believe his ears. Up until this very moment Orin hadn't given him any sort of lecture or advice on the subject of Olivia and the coming baby, even though Clancy had informed him of the situation. But now that his father was lying flat on his back in a hospital bed, he seemed to consider it the most important issue on his mind.

"Dad, now isn't the time for you to be worrying about me or Olivia. You—"

Before he could finish a nurse suddenly entered the room carrying a medicine cup filled with some sort of liquid.

"Sorry," she said briskly as she motioned Clancy toward the door. "Mr. Calhoun needs his rest. I'm sure Doctor Kennedy will allow him more visits tomorrow."

Grateful for the interruption, Clancy gave his father a quick goodbye and left the room, but as he stepped on the elevator to head down to the bottom floor, Orin's words continued to rattle through his thoughts.

You just make Olivia see that she needs to be a part of our family.

But how was he supposed to convince her? Clancy wondered. Even if he confessed how much he loved her, she wouldn't believe him.

Not now. She'd think his change of heart was all too sudden and convenient and he couldn't blame her. She couldn't possibly know that Clancy had never stopped loving her. It had just taken him too long to realize it.

The next morning, Olivia and Wes were getting ready to leave the office for a field trip when Bea entered the room with a small square of paper in her hand.

"Olivia, I have a message for you. I thought you might want to see it before you and Wes leave the office."

Wes winked at the secretary. "I'll bet it's more of the department heads begging her to take that promotion. The lady is in demand. We'll probably be seeing the last of her soon. She'll be basking in California warmth before the month is out."

Olivia frowned at him. "You're not going to

get rid of me that easily. I have no intention of taking the promotion."

Her announcement appeared to floor him and the young secretary. But Bea was the first to fully digest the news and the other woman actually jumped up and down with glee.

"You're not going to leave! Gee, that's great news, Livvy. Now when the baby comes I can be an auntie. And I'll babysit!" she added with a happy laugh.

Slower to respond, Wes looked at Olivia and shook his head with disbelief. "Do you realize what you're turning down? I'd give my eyeteeth for the chance you've been given. Why in the world aren't you going to accept it?"

Bea shot him a tired look. "Think for a minute, you big lug. It's like this, women follow their hearts. Unlike you men, they put love before money and position."

"Hey, don't jump on me." Wes attempted to defend himself. "I just want what's best for

Olivia. She's got a child to think of now. The new position would give her much more financial security."

"She'll have Clancy to help her with that," Bea put in as though Olivia couldn't speak for herself.

Rolling his eyes, Wes reached for his coat and hat. "Excuse me, but I haven't seen Mr. Calhoun around here for several days. Seems to me he's not all that interested in this coming baby."

"Wes!" Bea admonished. "You—"

Olivia stepped over to the secretary and patted her shoulder. "It's all right, Bea. Wes is right. Clancy hasn't been around. And most likely he won't be around. I sent him packing."

Bea's mouth fell open and then a frown of confusion came over her face as she looked down at the note in her hand. "Oh. Well, maybe you'd better look at this. Finn Calhoun called a moment ago. He said to give you this message."

She handed Olivia the small square of paper. "Finn? Are you sure about that?"

"He said his name was Finn."

Her mind whirling with questions, Olivia read the brief message, then let out a short gasp. "Oh, my! This says Orin, Clancy's father, is in the hospital." She looked frantically to Bea for answers. "Did Finn say what was wrong? Is his condition serious?"

Bea shrugged. "He said something about it being a heart attack. But the doctor hasn't told them exactly what's wrong yet. He said he thought you'd want to know. And that was basically all he said."

Dazed by the news, Olivia crammed the note in her coat pocket and was staring thoughtfully off in space when she felt Wes's hand on her sleeve.

"Livvy, if you think you ought to go to the hospital, we can put the field trip off to later in the day."

Olivia was shocked to feel tears stinging the backs of her eyes. She didn't know why this news of Orin had affected her so deeply. The two of them had chatted the night she'd attended Evan's birthday dinner and he'd been warm and kind to her, but other than that she'd not had a chance to really get to know him. But he was Clancy's father and that was enough to make the man special in her heart.

"It's nice of you to offer, Wes. But I think me saying a prayer for Orin will be better than showing up at the hospital."

Bea looked dumbfounded. "But, Livvy, what about Clancy? Don't you think he might need you now? That he might be glad to see you?"

She'd spent two years of her life watching her mother die a little each day and Clancy had never bothered to show his face or even call. True, when she'd ended their engagement she'd told him to move on and forget her. She'd told him to find someone else to love and start a family with. But deep down, she'd wanted him to refuse. She'd wanted to hear him say he loved her too much to let her go, that he loved her too much to allow her to care for her mother without his help. But he hadn't. And even after she'd gone back to Idaho, she'd waited and hoped he would show up on her doorstep and confess that he couldn't live without her. That had never happened and she seriously doubted it would happen now.

"I honestly don't know, Bea." Pulling her gloves out of her coat pocket, she glanced at Wes as she jammed her hands into the soft leather. She wasn't going to let herself think of Clancy or his father right now. If she did, she'd break to pieces. "Let's go. We've got work to do."

Chapter Twelve

Later that evening as Clancy stepped out of his father's hospital room, Finn was waiting out in the hallway and quickly pulled him to one side.

"How does Dad seem this evening?" he asked anxiously.

Clancy was the one who'd been chosen to spend the day at the hospital while the other men tended to work at the ranch and though his day had been long, he figured the hours had crawled by for his brothers, too, as they'd all been waiting for news from the doctor.

"Much better. Doctor Kennedy just left about five minutes ago. He says Dad's heart is fine. All the pain was coming from a stomach ulcer. He's already started Dad on medication for the problem and expects to release him from the hospital in the morning."

Finn let out a long sigh of relief. "That's great news. I was hoping to get here earlier, but one thing after another kept detaining me at the ranch. Rafe and Evan are on their way. Sassy's coming by as soon as Jett gets home to watch J.J. I guess now I can call and tell them all the good news."

Clancy nodded. "I just hung up from talking with Grandfather. He's mighty relieved."

"Well, this has hit the whole family pretty hard," Finn said. "I guess we've all wanted to think that Dad is invincible. Especially after we lost Mom. This incident has surely jerked the rug out from under my feet."

"It's hit me the same way," Clancy admitted, while pushing back his cuff and glancing at his watch. Even though the hour wasn't that late, he felt as though he hadn't slept in days. "Now that you're here I think I'll head on back to the ranch. It's been a long day."

"Yeah. I'm sure you're beat." Finn's gaze suddenly veered awkwardly away from Clancy's. "Uh, did Olivia come by today?"

Frowning, Clancy said, "No. Why would she? I've not told her about Dad."

"I did," Finn confessed. "At least, I left a message at her office. I thought she'd want to know. And I figured you'd be too stubborn to tell her."

A sick feeling hit the pit of Clancy's stomach. Apparently Olivia didn't care that he'd been worried sick over his father's health. She'd certainly not made any effort to contact him or show up at the hospital.

Maybe she's paying you back with some of your own medicine, Clancy.

Ignoring the accusing little voice in his head, Clancy shook his head. "So much for your thinking, Finn. Olivia doesn't care. And where do you come off always thinking you're some sort of matchmaker? Why can't you just leave people alone?"

That jerked Finn's head around and he glared at Clancy. "Well, excuse me for caring. And I'd hardly call it matchmaking. You and Olivia are having a baby together. You got matched without my help!"

Without saying another word, Finn stepped around him and entered their father's room.

Muttering a curse, Clancy walked to the nearest elevator and punched the down button. If he thought it would help, he'd head straight over to the Green Lizard and down enough margaritas to make his head buzz. But he doubted any amount of alcohol could blot out the agonizing thoughts going round in his head.

On the drive home, Clancy tried his best to simply focus on the traffic and the good news that his father would be well soon. But no matter how hard he tried to push Olivia and the baby out of his mind, the more they stuck there.

These past two weeks without her in his life had been a living hell for Clancy. Not being able to hold her close, to kiss and make love to her was like having parts of him torn away. No matter how hard he'd tried to keep his heart a safe distance from her, she'd found a crack and wiggled her way inside. Now more than anything, he missed talking with her and sharing the everyday happenings that had filled his days. She was a practical woman and he'd never realized how much she'd understood his needs and wants until she was gone.

When she'd turned down his proposal so vehemently he'd been angrier than he'd ever been in his life and that ire had simmered in him for days. She'd not been considering him or the baby, she'd only been considering herself. At least that's what his anger and pride had kept telling him. But slowly he was beginning to see that he'd run at her with the sensitivity of a raging bull. Now he didn't have a clue as to how to fix things with her. And he had to fix things. She and the baby were his family. The only family he'd ever wanted.

Once he arrived at the Silver Horn, he parked his truck at the back and entered the house by way of the kitchen. When he walked into the room, Greta was in the process of loading the dishwasher. She looked around at him and smiled with relief.

"I already got the word that Orin is going to be fine, but seeing you back home proves it to me." She straightened up from the dishwasher and rested her hands on her hips. "I'll bet you're plumb tuckered out. It's not easy sitting around a hospital for hours, worrying yourself silly."

He gave the cook a halfhearted smile as he shrugged out of his coat. "Don't worry about me, Greta. I'll get rested up. All that matters is that Dad is on the mend."

"I haven't put away the leftovers from dinner yet. Beef Stroganoff. I'll dish some up for you and put it in the warmer," she told him. "But first, you'd better go see Bart. He gave me orders to send you up as soon as you got home."

Clancy paused at Greta's side. "Grandfather wants to see me? I've already called and told him about Dad. What does he want?"

Greta let out a short laugh. "You think the old man would tell me? You'll just have to go up and find out for yourself. He's in his study. I'll have dinner waiting for you when you get back."

Clancy left the kitchen and climbed the stairs, but before he went to his grandfather's study, he stopped at his bedroom on the second floor to wash and change into a clean shirt. A few minutes later, he rapped on Bart's door and entered the cavernous room.

His grandfather was seated in a large armchair near the window. As Clancy approached, the other man lowered the book he'd been reading and peered over the glasses resting on his nose.

"Clancy, I know you're probably annoyed with me for summoning you tonight. But don't worry, I have no intentions of keeping you for long."

"I'm not annoyed." Clancy eased down in a chair angled to his grandfather's right elbow. "I'm sure you want to know more about Dad's condition. But frankly, I've already told you everything I know when we spoke on the phone."

Bart batted a hand through the air. "This isn't about Orin. I always knew my son was going to be fine. Hell, he's tougher than me and I'm still around. He's got years to go."

"Then what—"

Before Clancy could finish his question, Bart rose from the comfortable chair and walked over to a huge cherrywood desk where he plucked up a large, manila envelope.

Handing it to Clancy, he said, "Jett brought this to me this evening and I was anxious to pass it on to you."

Deciding it was probably a contract for the mineral rights Bart had been lobbying for over in Douglas County, Clancy pulled out the thick stack of papers. As he scanned the top page, he was swamped with tangled emotions.

"Grandfather, this is a deed! To me and Olivia!"

"You don't have to tell me what it is, Clancy. I had Jett draw it up. I've already signed it. Everything is in legal order. The twelve hundred acres up on Rock Mountain now belongs to you and Olivia. I suppose, if you like, you can still refer to it as Silver Horn land. But either way, you own it now."

Lost for words, Clancy dropped his head and rubbed a hand over his furrowed brow.

"Grandfather, it's been a few weeks since you first mentioned you were going to do this. A lot of things have happened since then," he finally said in a choked voice. "I'm not even speaking to Olivia now."

"Well, you sure as hell ought to be. She's going to give birth to your child. Along with that fact, she might like to know she's a new landowner. Free and clear."

Shaking his head, he looked at his grandfather. "I don't know what Dad or my brothers have told you, but Olivia doesn't want to marry me. I asked her and she turned me down. Emphatically, I might add."

No, Clancy, you told her. You didn't ask her. Not the way a man is supposed to ask a woman to be his wife for the rest of their lives.

Bart's impatient snort interrupted the mocking voice going on in Clancy's head.

"Maybe you didn't ask her right," Bart suggested. "And maybe you didn't make the effort to convince her that she'd fit in with the Calhoun family."

Confused now, Clancy watched Bart sink back into the armchair. "What do you mean, 'fit in'? Olivia isn't some shrinking violet. She's a strong woman. She'd never be concerned about fitting in with anyone anywhere."

Bart grimaced. "Really? Well, you should know her well. But I have my doubts that you do."

Irked by his grandfather's wisecrack, Clancy rose to his feet and walked over to the window. Down below he could see the yard lamps overlooking the mares' paddock and the big red connecting horse barn. Even now, at this late hour, the hands were still working, spreading hay and bringing the pregnant mares in for the night. The sight reminded him of the joy Olivia had expressed when Ezra had arrived with her horse, TR. Clancy could have easily gifted her a herd of twenty like the chestnut gelding, but she didn't want any part of his wealth or what it could give her.

"Maybe you're right, Grandfather. I don't know anymore."

"Clancy, women are hard to understand."

Clancy let out a loud groan. "Tell me something I don't know."

"All right. You might not believe it, but I had the dickens talking your grandmother into marrying me. She didn't want any part of being a rich Calhoun. That was her way of putting it. She was afraid she wouldn't fit in. She was afraid she would embarrass the family. She worried that she couldn't hold up to the standards of her in-laws. Ultimately, she didn't believe she was good enough to be my wife. Which was hogwash. I was the one who wasn't good enough for her. So I had to convince her that I loved her and would always love her no matter what."

As Bart's revelation slowly sank in on Clancy,

he glanced down at the deed he was still hold-ing in his hands. And suddenly Olivia's words were coming back to him. Words that she'd spo-ken when he'd confronted her about marrying someone else instead of coming to him.

Maybe someday you'll see that I'm not your kind. I never was and never will be... When you do finally marry, Clancy, you'll want your wife to be someone you can be proud of. You'll want her to be from a nice family.

Suddenly he was remembering back to their college days and how he'd felt when he'd met Olivia for the first time. Her dark, sultry looks had knocked him for a loop and so had her straightforward personality. He'd known im-mediately that she was going to be someone special in his life and he'd chosen not to reveal the fact that he came from a wealthy family. Instead, he'd simply told her that he lived on a ranch in northern Nevada and he'd figured that was enough. Otherwise, he might never really know if she was looking at him or merely impressed with his prominent background.

It wasn't until after they'd fallen in love and he'd slipped a diamond on her finger that Clancy had decided it was time to expose her to the truth. That's when he'd taken her home to the Silver Horn to meet his family. And now, thinking back on that time, he realized it was shortly after that visit when Olivia had told him she was returning to Idaho to be with her mother.

Looking up at his grandfather, he said, "I'm afraid you might be right, Grandfather. When I first met Olivia in college, I made a big mistake. I kept the fact that the Calhouns were wealthy from her for a long time, when I should have told her right off. And then after she learned the truth, I should've done a better job assuring her that the differences in our backgrounds made little difference. Now—well, I just don't know if I can be as persuasive with Olivia as you were with Grandmother."

Smiling now, Bart motioned him toward the door. "You've never disappointed me yet. Get gone, son."

Olivia poured the measure of grain into the feed trough, then stood beside the horse, stroking his neck as he munched on the pellets and corn coated with sweet molasses. At her feet, Pepper and Pete sat on their haunches watching and waiting for her attention.

"Okay, you three, I've got news for you," she said to the animals. "I've had a big chance at another job. If I'd taken it, you dogs could be eating steak and TR could get a fancy new saddle and ride around in a new horse trailer. But I turned the offer down. We're staying put. We're sinking our roots right here."

The dogs both tilted their heads to one side and whined with confusion.

"I know you don't understand," she said softly.

"I'm not sure I do, either. But that's the way it's going to be."

She'd worked tirelessly for nearly seven years to finish her education and reach this point in her career. To be offered such a position was a dream come true. But now that it had finally happened, she didn't want it. Clancy's baby meant far more to her than any job position or high-paying salary. She had no relatives to count on—how could she take this child away from his or her cousins and uncles and grandfather who'd spoil it?

From the time she was a little girl, she'd wondered why she couldn't live in a real family. One with a daddy and a mommy, who were happy and together. Instead, Chuck Parsons had left for greener pastures and, as soon as he'd been old enough, her brother, Todd, had done the same. After her mother had died, Olivia had married Mark out of loneliness and the belief that he truly loved her. But after only a few months into their marriage, he'd let her down, too.

She'd been disappointed and forsaken by the men in her life, but she desperately wanted things to be different for her child. More than anything she wanted this son or daughter she was carrying to be raised in a loving home, with a father who would always be there to guide and support his child. And there was no doubt in her mind that Clancy would be a dedicated father. But would he ever love and trust the mother of his child?

Once she'd made the decision to turn down the job promotion, she'd also come to the realization that she had to try again with Clancy. Somehow she had to convince him that she would never leave him for any reason and if she could manage that, then hopefully he would love her again.

Giving TR one last pat on his neck, Olivia hurried out of the stall, with the dogs at her heels.

She didn't know exactly where she might find Clancy tonight and her first inclination was to ring his cell phone or send him a text. But she didn't want to give him the chance to refuse to see her. She wanted to see him face-to-face, even if it meant she had to drive all the way to the Silver Horn or beyond. And once she made her feelings clear to him, she could only pray he was ready to give the three of them a chance to be a real family.

Thirty minutes later, Olivia had stepped out of the shower and was wrapping a heavy robe around her when she heard the dogs barking in the front yard.

Expecting to find Ezra at the door with a pot of antelope stew or some other dish he'd cooked for the two of them to share, she gasped when she peeped out the window to see Clancy standing on the threshold.

Oh, Lord, had Orin's health taken a turn for

the worst? Why else would he be showing up on her doorstep tonight? Her heart pounding, she jerked open the door and motioned for him to come inside.

"Clancy. Come in," she invited.

He stepped past her and the scent of cold wind and his spicy aftershave followed him into the house. More than a little dazed by his sudden appearance, she turned her back to him while she shut the door and fumbled with the lock.

A few steps behind her, he said, "I guess you're probably more than surprised to see me."

"Shocked is more like it." Olivia didn't add that she'd been about to dress and go in search of him. She wanted to hear what this visit was about before she confessed anything to this man.

"Sorry. I should have called first. But I—well, I was afraid you'd tell me not to come."

Incredibly, he'd been thinking the same as Olivia. So what did it mean? she wondered. That he'd changed his mind about her and the baby? About marriage?

Uncertainty caused her heart to lodge in her throat. "I wouldn't have done that."

"Thank you for that much," he said quietly.

Trying not to stand there gaping at him, she started out of the short foyer and he followed her into the living room. Thankfully, she'd started a fire earlier and now the space was warm and cozy.

After he'd removed his coat and hat and deposited them on a wall table, she motioned for him to join her on the couch. "Is this about your father?" she asked.

He eased down beside her and she couldn't keep her eyes off him. Like a half-starved animal, her gaze ate up the sight of his strong, masculine features and hard lean body dressed all in dark denim. These past couple of weeks she'd missed him desperately and had ached to feel his arms around her, to hear his low voice telling her how much he wanted her. Now that he was finally sitting here next to her, it felt a bit surreal.

"I understand Finn informed you about Dad being in the hospital," he said ruefully. "I'm sorry. I should've been the one to call you."

Was she hearing right? This wasn't the same Clancy who'd stormed out of her house two weeks ago.

"How is Orin?"

"Dad's going to be fine. In fact, he's going home tomorrow."

She let out a long sigh of relief. "I'm very glad to hear it."

His gaze slipped over the blue fleece robe she was wearing and the towel-dried hair lying in tangled waves upon her shoulders. "Were you about to go to bed or something?"

"I just got out of the shower and was about to dress when I heard the dogs barking." If possible her heart began to beat even faster. "Actually,

I was going to drive to the Silver Horn or the hospital. Wherever I could find you."

A shocked look came over his face. "You were? To find me? Why?"

Squaring her knees around so that she was facing him, she started to answer, only to have him stop her with a shake of his head.

"Wait," he said. "Before you say anything. I have something to show you."

Completely puzzled, she watched him leave the couch and go over to where his coat was lying on the tabletop. After pulling a manila envelope folded in half from the inside pocket, he walked back over to the couch and wasted no time in handing it to her.

"Grandfather gave this to me earlier this evening," he said. "I wanted you to see it."

Olivia pulled the contents from the envelope and quickly scanned the top of the beginning page. When she looked up at him, the shock she was feeling must have shown on her face because he reached over and clasped a hold on her forearm.

"Olivia, you've gone white. Are you okay?"

Without realizing it, one of her hands crept to her throat and she swallowed hard. "I don't understand any of this, Clancy. If you think I need something like this to persuade me to marry you, then—"

Shaking his head, he swiftly interrupted, "A couple of weeks ago, Grandfather wanted me to go with him up to the Rock Mountain range, so I drove him up there. And after we got there, he even wanted to hike down to the old mine."

Amazed at the idea of Bart making such a strenuous trek, Olivia asked, "Did he make it to the mine okay?"

"I had trouble keeping up with him," Clancy answered wryly, then shook his head as though he was just as amazed as Olivia. "It was while we were looking over the old mine that he told me what he was going to do with the land—that he wanted us two to have it. I was shocked. As shocked as you are now. He's never deeded any part of Horn land to any of the family before."

Olivia looked down at the deed. She was holding a small fortune in her hand, but it meant nothing without Clancy's love.

"You didn't tell me that Bart was planning to do this."

"I was going to. After you'd phoned me and asked me to come over—that we needed to talk. I was going to tell you all about it that night. But then you announced you were pregnant and the gift of the land hardly seemed an important issue. Especially after you told me you wouldn't marry me."

Releasing a long breath, she rose from the couch and stood with her back to him as she tried to collect her scattered emotions. "It's a nice gesture from your grandfather," she said huskily. "In fact, it's hard to believe that he'd want to do such a thing for me. But it's not—"

Suddenly he was standing behind her, his hands closing tightly over her shoulders and Olivia's heart was aching, yearning to hear the words she'd not heard from him in ten empty years.

"Olivia, it shouldn't be hard for you to believe. You're a wonderful woman. Bart wants you to belong to our family. He wants you to be a Calhoun almost as much as I do."

Hope and doubts were colliding and stumbling through her heart as she turned and rested her palms against his chest. "Because of the baby," she said lowly. "I can understand that, Clancy. But I—"

"Not because of the baby. Because I love you. And so does Grandfather, I might add."

"Love?" Not daring to believe she'd heard him right, she shook her head. "Do you know how long I've waited to hear you say that to me this time around and mean it? And now you conveniently come out with the words you think I want to hear."

His hand came up to gently cup the side of her face. "I don't deserve you, Olivia. After the way I've been behaving I can see why you'd doubt anything I say. But it's true. I don't think I ever stopped loving you. All those years we were apart—that was my fault."

"What do you mean?"

"When you went to help your mother through her illness, I should've followed you. I should've been there offering my help in any way I could. Instead, I went around nursing my crushed pride and expecting you to crawl back to me."

Groaning with regret, she turned away from him and walked over to the fireplace. As she stared unseeingly into the flames, she said, "All those years ago I was wrong, too, Clancy. I told you to forget me and start over, when all I really wanted was to beg you not to forsake me. I needed you desperately. But I didn't want to burden you. I loved you too much for that. I wanted you to go on with your studies. I wanted you to be happy and carefree. Not saddled with a poor fiancée and her dying mother. Still, I hoped and prayed that you'd ignore my wishes and come to Idaho anyway."

He came to stand by her side. "Is that why you married Mark? Because I never showed up or contacted you?"

Biting back a sob, she turned and reached for him and he pulled her tightly into his arms. "Oh, Clancy, after Mom died I felt so defeated and alone. I desperately needed someone in my life and it had been nearly three years since I'd left you and college behind and I'd not heard from you. Then Mark came along making a lot of promises and vowing that he loved me. I guess grief over losing you and Mom had clouded my common sense. I believed him. But we'd been married only a few short months when I realized it was never going to work. He didn't want me to finish my education. He didn't want me working for the BLM. He didn't want me doing anything except what he wanted."

His hand stroked the back of her damp hair. "I'm so sorry, Livvy. Sorry that I wasn't man enough to do the right thing all those years ago and that you went through a loveless marriage. But I'm especially sorry that these past few weeks I wasn't brave enough to admit to myself and you that I loved you. Even when my heart kept telling me otherwise."

Lifting her head away from his broad chest, she looked up at him. "I should tell you now, Clancy, that I've been offered a job promotion. It's a cushy position with a better salary and benefits. I'd be doing more work in the office than in the field and I'd have people working under me. The only catch is that the opening is in California. I'd have to transfer."

Clearly stunned by her news, his questioning

gaze traveled over her face. "A job promotion. So what is this going to do to us?"

"That depends on you," she told him.

His hands tightened on her shoulders. "Is this why you wanted to see me tonight? To tell me about the job?"

She shook her head. "No. I wanted to see you so that I could tell you how much I love you and that I'll never leave you no matter what. I've already turned down the job offer."

Her revelation had his head swinging back and forth in complete disbelief. "Turned it down? Olivia, have you thought this through?"

"I took one whole day. That was more than enough for me to decide that you and our baby are more important to me than any job. I want us to be together as a real family, Clancy. I want our child to be surrounded by our love and know that its home will always be solid and true."

"Oh, Livvy," he whispered, then swallowed hard. "I don't want you to sacrifice everything you've worked for. If you want to take the job in California, one of my brothers can take over my position as ranch manager. In fact, once Dad is over this stomach problem, he's more than capable of taking the reins again. We can move to California if that's what you want."

Her heart was suddenly brimming over with love and the joy of it was spilling through her, filling her with warmth and contentment. With all her doubts chased away, she lifted her hands to clasp his beloved face. No matter what the future brought to them, she was certain that Clancy would be there with her through the good and the bad.

"Oh, my precious darling, I would never allow you to do that. You belong on the Silver Horn. The ranch is more than your job, it's your home. Being its manager is what you were meant to be."

His eyes full of humble disbelief, he bent his head and rested his forehead against hers. "But your job is also important to you, Livvy," he murmured. "I want you to be happy."

She kissed one of his cheeks and then the other. "I will be happy, Clancy, with you and our children. And the job I have now is exactly what I want. Sitting behind a desk and telling other people what to do—that's not for me. I'd rather be hiking through the forest or wading through creeks."

A slow smile crept over his face. "You know, I think I honestly believe you."

Wrapping her arms around his waist, she hugged him tight against her. "You'd better believe me. Because you're going to be stuck with me for the rest of your life. Your family is going to be stuck with me." Easing out of his arms, she said, "Wait here. Don't move. I'll be back in just a moment."

She rushed out of the room and down the hallway to her bedroom. When she returned she was carrying the blue velvet box and the ring he'd given her more than ten years ago.

Handing it to him, she said softly, "I've kept this all these years, Clancy. Even when I desperately needed money, even when my ex-husband found it and threatened to hurt me if I didn't get rid of it, I held fast to the ring. It meant too much to me to ever let it go."

Humbled and dismayed, he slowly opened the little box and stared down at the teardrop diamond. "I can't believe this, Livvy. That you've held on to this ring all these years. Oh, God, I've been so wrong. So blind."

"We've both been wrong," she said gently. "But we're going to put our mistakes behind us and start anew. Do you think I can rightfully wear your diamond now?"

There was a slight shake to his hand as he pulled the ring from the velvet nest and slid it onto her waiting finger. The diamond winked back at her, as though the beautiful gem was now shining with true love.

"Oh, Livvy, all the time I was driving down here to see you tonight, I was expecting this talk with you to be hard as hell. I thought I was going to have to beg and plead and promise you everything to get you to agree to marry me."

He brought his lips down on hers and kissed her so tenderly that tears slipped from the corners of her eyes.

"And I thought it was going to take me a long, long time to earn your love and your trust. Now I'm wearing your ring again and I'll never take it off," she whispered against his lips. "You do trust me now?"

Slipping his arm beneath the back of her knees, he lifted her into the cradle of his arms. "Now and forever."

Her arms linked tightly at the back of his neck. "My bed has been very lonely these past two weeks. Think you can do anything about that?"

He let out a sexy chuckle as he carried her out of the living room. "Cleo is going to get an earful tonight."

Much, much later Olivia lay warmly nestled against Clancy's side with her cheek resting upon his warm chest. The night was getting late and she should've been drifting off to sleep, but joy and excitement was still buzzing through her. And how could she possibly get drowsy with Clancy's hand making slow seductive circles against her hip and the weight of his diamond on her finger kept reminding her of their future together.

Rising up to a sitting position, she said, "I think I'll get up and make us some hot chocolate. We still have a lot to talk about."

His hand was suddenly on her shoulder, pulling her back down to his side. "Not yet. I want you right here next to me. In a few minutes I'll get up and make the hot chocolate."

That had her gaze searching his face in the semidarkness of the bedroom. "My. You are full of surprises."

"That's right. And I have plenty more to show you."

Her fingers walked to the middle of his chest and tangled themselves in the patch of red-gold hair growing there. "I thought you already had."

Laughing softly, he turned on his side to face her, and Olivia's heart swelled with emotion as his hand settled against the lower part of her belly. Now that their future was clearly going to be spent together, the idea of carrying his baby was even more precious to her.

"Ever since you told me about the baby I've been envisioning him growing up on the ranch and learning all about cattle and horses and how to care for everything—to make it all work and last and keep going for the next generation. I also want to teach him how to love and be faithful and loyal. And I'll definitely need you to help me with that part," he said quietly.

Smiling, she caressed his cheek with her fingertips. "And what if we have a daughter?"

"Then I'll teach her all about ranching. My sister, Sassy, does all sorts of ranch work and does it well. So can our daughter. That is, if she wants to. Or she might want to follow in her mommy's footsteps and learn how to conserve and use the land. It'll be her choice. Or his choice. I want our children to grow up and follow their own passions. Even if it eventually takes them away from us. Giving a person choices and pride in his independence—you've taught me that loving is all about those things and more. Much more."

Amazed by his revelation, she said, "This probably sounds crazy, but I think your father's illness was a blessing in disguise."

"It certainly opened my eyes." He rested his lips against her forehead. "And showed me what really mattered to me. And that's you and our baby."

She eased her head back from his in order to look at him. "So now that your grandfather has given us the land for a home what am I going to do with this place?"

The patches of pale light drifting across his face revealed a broad smile. "We're going to keep it, of course. It's important to you. And it will be a nice place for us to come and stay on the weekends. We might even put a few more head of horses on it. I'm sure Ezra would be more than happy to look after things. Especially if I pay him a handsome salary. You think he'd want to hire out for us?"

"I imagine he would. But right now he's more interested in being the baby's godfather. He wants to be a part of its life. And I promised him that he would be. Is that okay with you?"

He hugged her close. "Darling, I wouldn't have it any other way."

He'd hardly gotten the words out when a thud suddenly shook the foot of the bed.

Lifting his head, Clancy glanced around the dark room. "What was that? A tremor?"

Olivia chuckled. "No. Cleo jumped on the foot of the bed. I guess she's finally decided you're worthy of her company."

"I knew that damned cat would finally come around. I just wasn't so sure about you, Livvy."

She pulled his head back down to hers and whispered, "Maybe I'd better convince you— one more time."

Epilogue

Three weeks later, on the first Saturday after Thanksgiving, Olivia and Clancy were married in a small but beautiful ceremony at the Calhoun family church. Incredibly, with the help of her two sisters-in-law, Olivia had found a beautiful pale pink dress with just enough gathers to drape over her barely burgeoning belly.

Beatrice had been thrilled to stand in as her maid of honor, while Sassy and Lilly acted as bridesmaids. Clancy had chosen Rafe to be his best man and though Orin was fully recovered from his stomach problem, he'd not been the one to walk Olivia down the aisle to give her away. Instead, she'd given that honor to Ezra, who'd taken it upon himself to be her stand-in father from the very first day she'd moved to Carson City. And as she walked toward the marriage altar with her hand on Ezra's arm, she realized that fate had not only brought her back to Clancy, it had also brought another special man into her life. One who she would always include in her family.

The reception afterward took place at the Silver Horn and though everyone was having a blast eating and dancing and making merry, Clancy somehow managed to sneak Olivia away from the crowd. After a quick change of clothes, they slipped out of the house and drove away before anyone realized they were missing.

"This is terrible," Olivia exclaimed. She glanced through the truck's back windshield to see the big three-story ranch quickly receding from her view. "Your family has put on such a wonderful party for us. And Bowie went to so much trouble to get a short leave to attend our wedding. He and the rest of the family are going to be angry with us for leaving."

Clancy chuckled as he gathered his new bride close to his side. "Don't worry. Bowie understands that I want to be alone with my bride. Besides, everyone will keep on having fun without us. And there'll be plenty more parties to be enjoyed. Now that Rafe and I are married things on the Horn have taken a definite change for the better. It's a happy place again." He leaned over and placed a quick kiss on her lips. "And you're part of the reason."

Smiling with sheer happiness, she looked down at the diamond on her finger and the small white wedding band resting beneath it. After years of being tucked away in her dresser, the ring was finally in its rightful place.

"So what are we going to do up in Reno? Got any surprises for me?" she asked slyly.

Because they'd both only taken a week off work for their honeymoon, the two of them had decided that a trip to nearby Reno would be more than enough to make them happy. And since Olivia had let Clancy make all the plans and reservations, she had no idea what he had in store for them these next few days.

"Oh, I've got a few plans up my sleeves." He shot her a promising grin. "But first I thought we'd drive by our land up on Rock Mountain. Do you mind?"

"I'd love to." She glanced with misgiving down at her sweater dress and knee-length high-heeled boots. "But I'm not exactly dressed for climbing up to the meadow."

"I threw your old boots in the backseat," he informed her. "And if you soil your dress, I'll buy you a new one."

She laughed. "I'll take you up on that."

Twenty minutes later, Clancy drove as far as he could to the top of the mountain property and then they hiked the remaining distance to the meadow.

As they stood side by side, gazing out at the opening, Clancy slipped an arm against her back and hugged her close. "Cold?" he asked.

"No. I was imagining how wonderful it will be to live up here with our children."

"I already have a contractor picked out to do the ground excavation and build the house," he told her. "As soon as we get back from our honeymoon I'm going to contact him and tell him to start as soon as possible. Then you and I will look at the plans the architect drew up and choose just the house we want. This time next year we'll be able to stand in the living room, look out over the mountaintop and show our baby its legacy."

Looking up at her husband, she couldn't help but think about all the bumps, setbacks

and lonely years she'd endured before she'd become Clancy's wife. There had been times she'd
nearly given up on finding love and even more
times she'd called herself a fool for hanging on
to Clancy's ring. But since then she'd learned a
very important lesson. Some dreams could actually come true. She was living hers now.

"What about the old mine?" she asked. "What
are we going to do with it?"

"First thing, I'm going to have a security fence
erected around the hole for safety reasons," he
said. "After that, I'd like to know your ideas on
the subject. What would you like to do with it?"

She glanced down the mountain to where
they'd discovered the dammed lake and nearby
opening to the mine. "We don't know whether
the hole in the side of the mountain is full of
gold or silver. Or if the whole cavern is worthless. And I don't think that part of it even matters. It was once full of hopes and dreams and,
in my opinion, that in itself is a fortune. Let's

give the mine to our children and in years to come, they can decide whether they want to re-open it or not."

"Somehow I knew you'd say that."

He kissed her for long moments, his lips full of love and promises. Then the two of them walked hand-in-hand down the mountain to begin their honeymoon and the rest of their lives together.

* * * * *